KEMI'S
JOURNAL

of life, love and everything

ABOUT THE AUTHOR

Abidemi Sanusi is a human rights worker and writer. She was born in Nigeria and now lives in the UK. A keen runner, Abidemi is also the editor of www.christianwriter.co.uk. You can find out more about Abidemi on her personal website www.abidemi@christianwriter.co.uk.

DEDICATION/ACKNOWLEDGEMENTS

This book is dedicated to my father: Abdul Rasaak Olajide Sanusi; not a day goes by when I don't think about you. And to the Holy Spirit; this book is for You. We did it!

And special thanks to my mother: I wouldn't ask for another. My gratitude to everyone who's made this book possible – you know who you are.

All characters in this book are entirely fictitious.

KEMI'S JOURNAL

of life, love and everything

ABIDEMI SANUSI

KEMI'S JOURNAL

Published by Scripture Union,
207-209 Queensway, Bletchley, MK2 2EB, UK.

Scripture Union: Scripture Union is an international Christian charity working with churches in more than 130 countries providing resources to bring the good news about Jesus Christ to children, young people and families – and to encourage them to develop spiritually through the Bible and prayer. As well as a network of volunteers, staff and associates who run holidays, church-based events and school Christian groups, SU produces a wide range of publications and supports those who use the resources through training programmes.

Email: info@scriptureunion.org.uk
Internet: www.scriptureunion.org.uk

British Library Cataloguing-in-Publication Data: a catalogue record for this book is available from the British Library.

Quotations from the New International Version of the Holy Bible, © 1973, 1978, 1984 by International Bible Society, used by permission of Hodder and Stoughton Limited.

Cover design and photography by Phil Grundy
Internal design and typesetting by EH Graphics of E Sussex, UK
Printed and bound in Great Britain by Creative Print and Design (Wales) Ebbw Vale

KEMI'S JOURNAL
of life, love and everything

Wednesday March 6

... seek first his kingdom and his righteousness... (Matthew 6:33).

I have decided to keep a diary this year. You know, kind of like a spiritual diary. Never mind the fact that we're already way into the New Year. Everyone tells me about the utmost importance of doing this. OKAY... maybe not everyone. Triple S People (Spiritual Super Stars) tell me it's vital to keep track of what God is doing in my life.

Personally, I don't know what the big deal is about the New Year, anyway. Sure, I do distinctly recall kneeling by my bed at the year end, praying in my desires. But, as far as I can see, nothing's changed. It's hard to live for God and make the heavenly kingdom my concern when my life is a glitzy advertisement for Boring Inc.

Mum called today. *Was I alright?*

'Of course I'm alright,' I squelched down the phone.

'Just checking,' she said. 'It's just I worry about you. You're not getting any younger, you know. You're 28 and you don't have any fun. All that going to church. When was the last time you shook your boogie and really enjoyed yourself?'

Shook my boogie?

'Mum, I'm fine. Stop worrying. You know, if you would come with me to church one day, you might just enjoy it.'

'Not me. Why you waste your time with those holy rollers, I'll never know. Filling your head with nonsense. Absolute nonsense! Got to go. Love you. Byeee.'

Love you too, mother.

Promised myself that the next time I would have the last word. Though she does have a point about my life – or lack thereof.

Hey! What am I thinking? I'm a born again Pentecostal Christian!

Same day, that afternoon

Had a call from Zack, the boyfriend from life BC (Before Church). I'm sure Mum called him. I must be the only woman blessed with an ex-boyfriend who can do no wrong as far as her parents are concerned. Anyway, I don't know why he bothers. You would think a year's long enough for anyone to understand that you're not interested in them. Anyone but Zack, it seems. He just doesn't seem to get the message.

Zack rocks though.

Dear God, there must be more to this Christianity stuff than going to church, prayer meetings and conventions. I'm turning into the person I promised myself I would never be – the boring church girl who needs to get a life.

Thursday March 7

Have mercy on me, O Lord, for I call on you all day long (Psalm 86:3).

Dear Lord, I need all the help I can get. Feel like I'm slipping.

The day didn't start too well. Spotted a fine-looking specimen at the bus stop this morning. Didn't realise I was staring until the woman beside him screeched, 'What are you looking at?' I ignored her. Didn't want anyone thinking we were both crazy. But the bloke winked at me as he got on the bus. I ignored him and took out my Bible. You never saw a smile disappear so fast.

Then Zack called me. As if I wasn't stressed out already. The devil sure knows how to pick his agents. Wanted us to meet for lunch. Refused. It's that time of the month. Don't trust my hormones. I just wish he would leave me alone. Thinking of the Bible verse for the day from my daily devotional comforted me somewhat. If the Psalmist could feel like that, then I guess it's okay to feel like this. And like him, I'm calling on you, God, to steady me. I'm starting to feel like church is stealing my joy.

There's a prayer meeting tonight. Not sure I really want to be there. All that noise. One would think God was deaf.

Still three hours to 5.30. I'm in the toilet writing this. I'm not cut out for work. Or maybe it's just marketing I'm not cut out for.

Vanessa, my perfect best friend, just sent a text. She wants us to go shopping after work. I just don't know if I can face hearing more about her perfect fiancé, Mark. Then she'll turn to me and say, 'Don't worry. God is faithful. If I can be engaged, then God can do the same for you.'

At home, that evening

Had a lovely time with Vanessa. She really cheered me up. Zack called when I got home. We're going to Smollensky's jazz club this weekend. Will definitely cancel. I know God definitely tut-tutted when I said, 'Yes!' At least I have a date other than meeting up with Vanessa. I really must make more of an effort with relationships. Tell you what, I'll go evangelising. What better way to make friends?! (Or enemies?)

Lord, what am I going to wear to Smollensky's? I saw the bus-stop guy again on my way home. Minus girlfriend. He didn't smile at me. As if I care. *I'm going to Smollensky's!*

Friday March 8

I can do everything through him who gives me strength (Philippians 4:13).

Thank God it's Friday. Tomorrow, I'm going to pop into the gym, head down to the hairdresser's and afterwards get a pedicure. I'm still planning to cancel with Zack. But, there again, what's wrong with wanting to go and hang out with a friend at a jazz club?

But he's an ex.

That doesn't mean anything.

You still have feelings for him.

Feelings don't matter. I'm strong. Like the apostle. I can do everything through Christ who strengthens me. Except keep my eyes focused on getting ready for work. MOVE IT GIRL!

Actually Zack called late last night. I saw his number on caller ID. I didn't pick up. I just knew he was going to make a big deal about our date – or rather our get-together (that's better). That boy needs prayer.

And I need deliverance. It's a soul tie thing. And I need to break it. Can I imagine myself going to my pastor? 'I need to break soul ties with my ex so I can be free to move on.'

I pictured the pastor laying hands on my head, tilting it, and holding it back at an awkward angle with the confidence of a man used to exercising authority over devils.

'In the name of Jesus! Break free! Free! Who the Son sets free is free indeed! May the blood of Jee-esus cleanse you from demonic ties... '

Yes, think I'll take a rain check on that.

Don't want to go to work though. Think I should call in sick?

Lunch break

I just knew I shouldn't have come in today. The one weekend I have a date (sorry, get-together) and I have to go to Paris for the weekend.

'Why can't Robert do it?' I asked Amanda. She's the Executive Marketing Director and my boss. And Robert sits at the desk next to me, which is unfortunate because he's got a pretty bad body-odour problem.

'You're going and that's that. Don't be difficult,' she said. She's the one that's so difficult. An agent from Beelzebub himself. I get all the dumb campaigns. It was me who got the water-inflated bras. And the organic spring water. And the revolutionary new lawn mower. And the assertiveness training weekends in Bognor Regis. And now it's the musical nappies. What a daft idea. God, why am I doing this job? OH GOD! I HAVE TO CALL ZACK AND CANCEL OUR DATE (GET-TOGETHER)! He'll definitely hate me, for sure. He'll probably think I'm lying.

3pm

Had a word with Amanda. Told her I wasn't feeling well.

'I don't care if you're the living dead,' she said. 'You're going and that's it. It's only a weekend, for Gawd's sake!' Now I know what my mission is: to pray for that woman. Don't know why I missed it before. Smollensky's doesn't matter. I haven't had a date for a year. I haven't had a social life for a year either. But who cares! I have Jesus!

So why do I feel like I can't be bothered with my faith anymore? It suddenly came to me! I'm under spiritual attack from the Evil One. But I can do all things through Christ. I'm strong. I'm a born again demon-kicking, Spirit-filled Pentecostal believer! Beat that, devil!

Checked my email. My cousin Foluke will be in London next month. She has issues. I used to describe her as neurotic but I was being politically correct. She's not neurotic. She's an absolute nutter.

5pm

Home. Called Zack and started to tell him about things and he hung up on me. Great! Paris won't be so bad really as I won't be working all the time – just a couple of hours tomorrow and Sunday thrashing out the client's advertising campaign. Don't know why Amanda couldn't have sorted this out a long time ago. Can I fit in a manicure tonight before I get the Eurostar?

Saturday March 9

When you walk through the fire, you will not be burned; the flames will not set you ablaze (Isaiah 43:2b).

Didn't get my nails done. Zack came round just as I was closing my front door to go out. I ran back into the flat when I saw him but he threatened to break the door down if I didn't let him in, so I had to really. It felt sort of nice that he thought it was so important.

What am I thinking?!

Anyway, he came in, sat on my sofa and put his head in his hands. He's got lovely hands. He said, 'Why did you cancel?'

I tried to explain. 'I have to go to Paris. Sorry.'

'Bit sudden, isn't it?'

'You know what Amanda's like. Anyway, I just have to go.'

'Where're your bags?'

'I'm popping out for a quick manicure first.'

'Are you or are you not going to Paris?'

'I am. But first I need a manicure. Please leave! I don't want to be late.'

'If you didn't want to go out with me, all you had to do was say.' He left.

I felt so low. Can't believe the guy still has the power to affect me like this even after a year of not being with him. If he was a Christian, we would sail into the marital sunset but no, he doesn't see the point of my faith. And what's the point of getting involved with someone who isn't interested in the most important thing in your life? Just wished he wasn't so... so *perfect* though.

I didn't have the manicure after all. Felt so despondent after Zack left, I cried and totally indulged in a reassuring bout of self-pity. For ages. I'm boyfriendless. Unlike all my friends. Plus my faith feels unreal. Plus I can't stand my job and my boss is Beelzebub's daughter. With all these pressures, is it any wonder I'm cracking up?

I kept thinking, if I could just see Jesus in person, I would be okay. It really would make all the difference. I'm just not a good advertisement for this faith thing. Maybe if I had a fantastic testimony about seeing Jesus or angels or heaven, maybe I wouldn't struggle so much. Not much point in walking through fires à la today's Bible verse when I would rather be delivered from them.

But I digress.

Self-pity marathon lasted 30 mins which left me another 30 mins to pack my bags and get myself to the station to catch Eurostar. By the time I was stuffing too much into my overnight bag I was starting to panic and worry about Friday night traffic big time. Then my phone rang.

'I thought you were going to Paris?' It was Zack.

'Yes, but I'm late and there's just no way I'll get to Waterloo on time.'

'I'm outside. I'll take you to the station. Sorry about being such a pain. I knew you were telling the truth. It's just that I was really looking forward to Smollensky's.'

'No problem,' I said, before flying out of the flat. Thank You Lord!

2pm

Late lunch break. Meeting going OK. I think. There's Windy CEO – he passes wind relentlessly – from Singing Diapers UK subsidiary and his equally smelly Head of Marketing. (His particular problem's more in the area of nervous body odour, even worse than Robert's.)

The diapers are going to be launched in a few weeks and we don't even have the beginning of an advertising campaign. How did this happen? What was Amanda thinking? Most importantly, will I get any sleep in the next couple of weeks bearing in mind the advertising situation (or lack thereof) for this product?

Windy CEO has been coming up with the most ludicrous ideas.

'Aliens! What if we feature the diapers as friendly aliens from outer space who tell toddlers when they're wet?'

Smelly bobs his head feverishly. 'Fantastic!'

'Or we could come up with a cartoon with the diapers as the lead characters. Sort of diapers with minds.'

'Wonderful. Yes, wonderful!' More frantic bobs from Smelly.

I *determined* to bring this under control.

'What if we go for a simpler advertising campaign? You, know... research shows that mothers are tired of gimmicks. If we just market the diapers for what they are without insulting people's intelligence, then surely, that would sell more, wouldn't it?'

Silence. Then Windy CEO asked, 'What do you have in mind?'

'Well, these are the diapers that alert parents by playing musical notes when toddlers have wet themselves. No more guesswork for harassed, busy parents. After all, it's the parents who buy diapers – not the toddlers.'

Windy CEO claps. 'Wonderful!'

Smelly starts bobbing, then gets a crick in his neck.

All in all, a very satisfactory ending. Nothing to it really. Diapers should be marketed as diapers. Marketing them any other way would be stupid. It's times like this that I really appreciate my job. It's about helping people. Giving them choices and making their lives that much easier.

6pm

That serpent, Smelly! The whole weekend's ruined. Just had a phone call from Amanda. She was livid. Said Smelly said I wasn't cooperative and that I'd practically forced my idea down everybody's throat! And that the CEO had changed his mind and was sticking to the Martian concept.

Tried to defend my approach but couldn't get a word in.

Thing is, there's a dinner with Smelly et al this evening. Lord, re today's Isaiah promise feel free to douse this fire with water at any time. Just in case you hadn't noticed, I'M IN TROUBLE!

Sunday March 10

Give thanks to the LORD, for he is good; his love endures for ever (Psalm 118:1).

On Eurostar heading home. Prayed after my last entry. Don't know if 'prayed' is the right word. More like I flung myself at God and bawled for wisdom. Then calmed down and went to dinner. What do you think? Windy CEO came right up to me as I arrived, said he'd changed his mind again, that he preferred my idea. Said I was right, that we should target the people with purchasing power. Asked me to head their next campaign, too. Spied Smelly glowering at me from the corner of my eye. I smiled at him. Sweetly. Not sure how Amanda will feel about me grabbing the next campaign. Don't want her to think I'm trying to wrestle her job from her... which I am, of course.

Tuesday March 12

... be strong in the Lord and in his mighty power (Ephesians 6:10).

Amanda's still not speaking to me. Office atmosphere rather

uncomfortable. As if I *asked* Windy CEO to give me the next product campaign. He's insisting I head it – not Amanda. As if my life wasn't complicated enough.

Saw bus-stop man again today. Minus girlfriend. Wonder what's happened? I said hello to him and took out my Bible as we both sat down on the bus. He was seated directly opposite me. Saw him look at me when he thought I wasn't looking.

Vanessa called. Wants to come round after work. Told her I was having a manicure. 'Me too!' she said. Guess I'm stuck with her. I just want some time to myself. Is that too much to ask?

10pm

Guess what? We bumped into Mum at *Tutti Beauty* having her nails done. She's so well preserved it's disgusting. We went for coffee, ate too many chocolate chip muffins and had a lovely time actually – three women just chilling out. I love my Mum. She's cool. Dad's cool too. They're both cool. Vanessa sometimes gets on my nerves, though. Mark's been elevated to god status.

Friday March 15

I will sing to the LORD all my life; I will sing praise to my God as long as I live. May my meditation be pleasing to him, as I rejoice in the LORD (Psalm 104:33,34).

Thank God for Fridays! I'm going to go home, get changed and go to the prayer meeting. I've missed God so much! What with Zack, Paris and Amanda, he's been pushed onto the back burner.

Midnight

Thank you, Jesus, for your love and peace. The minute I walked into the prayer meeting, I was just... you know... aware of you. Thank you for your free gift of salvation. I know I'm not the most perfect Christian in the world but your presence in that room showed me you did love me even if I'm not perfect. The best Friday present ever.

Sunday March 17

... all things are possible with God (Mark 10:27).

Pastor Michael preached on *Settling for Second Best.* That's it. I'm going to hand in my resignation tomorrow. Amanda et al can all jump, as far as I'm concerned. I knew the job wasn't what God ordained for me. I'm destined for better things. I'm meant to soar like an eagle.

(I'm also meant to get a mortgage on a five-star studio flat and get married – to Zack preferably – in a Tiffany dress... but I digress again.)

I'm going to go for it. I'm going to go out in the streets and evangelise. The whole world shall know of the saving power of Jesus Christ. Even Zack? Yes, even him! Even though it's a damp spring and freezing outside. The whole point is this: I don't ever have to settle for second best because God sent his very best to die for me. Why should I settle for scraps?

Monday March 18

... no weapon forged against you will prevail, and you will refute every tongue that accuses you (Isaiah 54:17).

Amanda called me into her office and apologised for her behaviour last week. 'You should be sorry,' I wanted to say. 'You messed up the Singing Diapers account and when you couldn't fix it, you sent me along to Paris but God delivered me and you couldn't hack it.'

But I didn't. Instead I smiled sweetly and said, 'It's okay.' I didn't know what else to say so I left her office. Tad uncomfortable actually.

Wednesday March 20

Ask and it will be given to you; seek and you will find; knock and the door will be opened to you (Matthew 7:7).

Mum's in hospital. She's had a stroke.

Wednesday March 27

... do not worry about tomorrow, for tomorrow will worry about itself. Each day has enough trouble of its own (Matthew 6:34).

What a week since I last wrote in my journal!

My Dad (he's called Femi) is not taking this very well. He's a bank manager. Mum (Gail) manages a local charity shop. They've been married for 30 years. They got married when they were both 16. Dad's black and Mum's white. To explain a bit: my grandfather on my mother's side was a colonial officer in Lagos, Nigeria. My father's mother was a maid in their house. My parents were playmates who woke up one morning and decided to get married. Naturally when they got to the registry office, my mother's father was alerted. Needless to say, my mother found herself on the next plane to England. My father wasn't the kind to give up easily. Beatings and threats notwithstanding, he stole into a ship destined for England. He was found at Liverpool, emaciated and an inch from death. He appeared in the newspapers the next day, which was how Mum tracked him down.

They got married two weeks later. Mum was disowned by her family but she didn't care. It was the 70s and they were having fun. Romantic or what? I am the result of that beautiful union, and now Mum's had a stroke. I don't know how Dad will cope. God, why this? Why now?

Friday March 29

Therefore keep watch, because you do not know the day or the hour (Matthew 25:13).

Mum's okay. Her condition's stabilised. Had the church prayer team come and pray for her. Pastor Michael even laid the dreaded hands on her. Dad didn't complain. I guess he was too desperate. He's aged. We both have this week.

Monday April 15

He has made everything beautiful in its time. He has also set eternity in the hearts of men; yet they cannot fathom what God has done from beginning to end (Ecclesiastes 3:11).

Lord, how merciful art thou! Thank you for sparing my mother. I've done a lot of thinking over the last few weeks, even though I somehow didn't get around to writing it down. It wasn't so much the fact that I faced life without my mum that terrified me. It was the knowledge that I could face the *next* life without her that drove me to my knees to pray some pretty desperate prayers.

It's true. One minute you're here and the next you could be gone like the wind.

Mum's doing okay now. She's back home, thank God. She told me she sensed our prayers when she was in hospital. 'But I'm still not coming to your church,' she added. When I started talking to her about Jesus, Dad rushed me out of the room with the words, 'I will not let you kill your Mum after the doctors have delivered her.' But he winked at me. I smiled. My parents are back.

But so is Zack.

He's been great the last couple of weeks. I honestly don't know what I would've done without him.

I tried so hard to keep him away. Lord, you know how weak I am. Actually, Dad called him about Mum and asked him to keep an eye on me! He didn't know he was sending his daughter to the lion's den. I tried, Lord. I really tried to keep Zack away. Thing is, I'm still in love with him. He came round two nights ago. Vanessa had just left. The strain of it all was too much and I just burst into tears.

He just held me and told me everything was going to be okay and the next thing I know, we're kissing. And then we slept together.

The phone's ringing. It's Zack. His number's on caller ID. I don't want to talk to him. I need to think. *Focus, Kemi, focus.*

I've just yanked the phone out of the socket and switched off my mobile. The noise was driving me crazy. Maybe he'll get the message.

I will not think about God. *Mustn't.*

Tuesday April 16

Everyone has heard about your obedience, so I am full of joy over you; but I want you to be wise about what is good, and innocent about what is evil (Romans 16:19).

1am

Okay, I've thought this through. No one has to know. I fell off the wagon but, at the end of the day, it's between me and God. I think. I'll tell Vanessa, though. She's my best friend and I really need someone to talk to. She'll understand. And I know she won't judge me for saying the sex even felt good. Or will she? Jesus, what have I done? Okay, don't bring Jesus into this. You *knew* what you were doing, Kemi, so don't start crying over spilt milk. I feel wretched. Just wretched.

3.30am

Just got off the phone from Vanessa. I burst into tears and told her everything. She was so kind. Dear Lord, I am sorry for all the times I misjudged her. Actually, I wish I was more like her. Strengthen me, Jesus. She said I shouldn't *fraternise* with Zack anymore. That I should cut all my links with him, even changing my number if necessary. She said I should go for a deliverance session, 'to cut every spiritual bond that is not from the throne room of heaven.' Whatever. I really, really hate it when she starts displaying all the hallmarks of Triple S. I'm not demonised, am I? Zack is not the devil incarnate, is he? We made a mistake. That does not make me a terrible person. Oh, Jesus, I've messed up big time.

8.45am

Late for work. Don't want to go in but have to. Taken too much time off in the last few weeks. Bet Amanda will be happy. Witch that she is. I'm sorry. She's not a witch. She's a cherub. You see, this is what sin is doing to my mind. But then, how sane can I be, heading up an advertising campaign to sell musical nappies?

12.45pm

I'm in the loo at work. Can't concentrate. I keep on thinking of the Holy Spirit and what a disappointment I must be to him. Then I think of Zack and how it's not fair that he should be treated this way. I still haven't spoken to him. It's not right. He hasn't done anything. I'm the one that's done this and he should know *why* we cannot pursue it anymore. The most perfect man in the whole world and I can't have him because he doesn't share my beliefs. It really sucks. He doesn't even understand the whole 'born again' thing. I've tried so hard to explain it to him. He still doesn't get it. The way I read it, the Bible makes it clear that believers in Christ Jesus as Lord and Saviour have no business being this intimate with non-believers, agnostics and whatever else is out there. Is that right? The thing is, Zack is not a bad person. He's the kindest, sweetest guy I've ever known – or probably will ever know, seeing as I'm booking myself into a convent at the earliest opportunity.

I'm tired. Vanessa's called me 50 times already today. 'I think you should go and see Pastor Michael,' she said. Yeah, right! The last thing I want is for anyone to make my life a sermon item. I'm being mean. He's not like that. I'm still not seeing him, though. He's a pastor, for crying out loud! He's also a human being with a ten-foot halo. I'm not seeing him. What for? I had a temporary aberration. Just the one time. It doesn't make me an adulteress. It won't happen again so I do not need to see Pastor Michael. I'm tired and I need to sleep.

I must call Zack.

No, I mustn't. What I need to do is get my *derrière* home and pray for forgiveness. Again. Just in case God didn't hear me wailing this morning. I'm going to wise up to what's good and what's evil and sort myself out.

Have to get back to my desk. Have a meeting with Smelly re the diapers TV ads. I think I'll go and see Mum and Dad after work. I want them to tell me that everything is okay. That I'm not a bad person. Not that I'll ever tell them what happened, of course. We're close, but they're still my parents.

8pm

In the loo. At home. Zack's here. He was waiting outside my office when I finished work. I'm still so weak. When I saw him standing there in his barrister suit (minus wig, of course) my heart leapt. *Get thee behind me, devil!* But I wasn't going to make a scene and we have to talk so here we are.

Vanessa's here as well. I didn't know how to explain Zack's presence so here I am. In the loo. All very dignified really.

Thursday April 18

In the same way, the Spirit helps us in our weakness. We do not know what we ought to pray for, but the Spirit himself intercedes for us with groans that words cannot express (Romans 8:26).

Thank God for today's Bible verse! It's good to be back close to the Lord. I've had a rethink in the last couple of days. Hiding myself in my own loo in my own flat was the last straw. Yes, I've indulged in pre-marital sex – but I've repented. *As far as the east is from the west, so far has he removed our transgressions from us.* That's what the Bible says. Sex before marriage is not God's best. I know that, but it happened and now I have to move on. As I sat in that loo, it was like a light went on in my head. I got off the toilet seat, marched into the living room and announced, 'I'm sorry, but the two of you have to go. I'm tired and I haven't had a good night's sleep in two days.' I disappeared into the shower before they could reply and, by the time I came out, they were both gone. I went to bed and fell asleep immediately.

Vanessa's not talking to me but I know she'll come round. As for Zack, I called yesterday and told him exactly what I'd rehearsed in my mind: 'I'm sorry. What happened shouldn't have, but it stops there. I know I've hurt you and I'm sorry but please don't call me again.' And I hung up the phone. He called me all day yesterday, but hasn't called me today. I think he's got the message.

God is in control. I can do this. I have the Holy Spirit. He will help me in my weakness. I just hope Zack's okay. He doesn't deserve to be treated like this.

Sunday April 21

I will walk among you and be your God, and you will be my people (Leviticus 26:12).

Spent the weekend at Mum and Dad's. Mum seems pretty much recovered. They're so funny! I love it when they tell me stories of how Mum found Dad in hospital in Liverpool. A real life love story and so romantic. Shame we don't have many of those nowadays. My cousin from Dad's side, Foluke, was there too. I've told you about her. She's 35 and very confused.

Actually, she went into therapy last year. She needs it. She's off her rocker. Not that I should be pointing at the speck in her eye, being a sexual relapse myself and everything (read: redeemed sexual relapse: *whom the Son sets free is free indeed*. I must remember that).

I'm digressing again.

Anyway, she had one of those regressive hypnotherapy thingies. Get this: turns out that she was 'abused' when she was a child and – this is where it gets even stranger – at the end of the session she decided to 'come out' because the experience revealed the truth of her 'fascination with women and the things that can progress us in the way of the ancient goddesses'. I told her to shut up.

Turns out she believes that God made Adam and Eve but, 'that doesn't explain the life cycle of humans as we progress through the many rhythms of life'. And I thought I had problems. She told me her parents think they've done something to offend God because he's given them a daughter like her. I told them that a lot of parents think that way about their kids. But they don't, believe me. (I was just being kind.) What do I know anyway? I'm of mixed parentage. There's enough stuff in there to keep a therapist in business for life.

Back to my parents. I absolutely love and adore them. Thank you, Jesus, for giving them to me. I pray I have a marriage like theirs. Well, they've been married for 30 years so I guess they've had a long time to get used to each other. I used to resent being an only child but, in retrospect, it's a good thing. I have my parents all to myself.

Except I had to leave their house early today because Zack was coming round for dinner. God, I really hope the man you have in store for me wins my parents over something like he has. They truly believe Zack cannot do anything wrong.

However, I'm sure Mum knows something's up with me. She has a radar NASA would pay zillions of pounds for.

Monday April 22

The man of God replied, 'The LORD can give you much more than that' (2 Chronicles 25:9).

The skulduggery continues at the office. Amanda and Robert

have joined forces. I see them going for cigarette breaks and having drinks together after work. But they can't stand each other! Once I went into Amanda's office and Robert was there. They both stopped talking and looked at me as if to say, 'yeah?' Seems the battle lines have been drawn and I wonder who'll be the last person standing.

Saw my bus-stop friend. We were both running for the bus. Actually, three of us were running for the bus. His 'other half' was also in the marathon. I said, 'Wow!' when we all caught it and smiled at her and she completely ignored me. The Jezebel spirit has taken permanent residence in her. The boyfriend smiled back though. I quickly moved away from them. I didn't want her scratching my eyes out. What was her problem, anyway? Crikey. Londoners are so highly strung. They need Jesus.

Lord, I miss Zack. I'm trying so hard to be strong.

Be still and know I am the Lord.

If I could just see you for one minute, Jesus, just one minute, I know I'd be okay.

I am always with you, even to the end of the age.

Seeing you would be better. Much better. All this faith stuff. What's it all about anyway? I don't know what I'm doing. I've been a Christian for a year. I haven't brought anyone to faith in you. I'm still in love with my ex-boyfriend – who I had sex with last week. And I'm trying very hard not to think about how good (not good, *great*) it was. And can I just remind you of my work situation? EVERYONE HATES ME!! They all think I'm a campaign-snatcher! What a mess! What do you even see in me anyway? I'm not perfect like Vanessa. That's probably why you gave her a lovely fiancé, because she's perfect.

I'm sorry. I hate it when I descend into self-pity. You see what I mean, Lord? I'm useless! Wars, AIDS, child abuse – and all I can think about is myself.

I know what I'm going to do. I'll call Foluke. Let's see if this 'ministering to others when you're down' business really works. Foluke's been trying to hang out with me all week but I've refused. Emotional, mental, spiritual and hormonal imbalance reasons and all that. And the fact that I would in all likelihood want to hurl myself over a cliff once I leave her presence. She's so depressing.

She needs you.

I know, Lord, but what about *my* needs?

You know me.

Fine. I'll call her. We'll hang out but don't be surprised if I turn up at the pearly gates when we're done.

Thursday April 25

In God, whose word I praise, in God I trust; I will not be afraid. What can mortal man do to me? (Psalm 56:4).

Jesus, how did you know how things would turn out? We had a great time on Monday night and guess what? We prayed! That was all! I got there and Foluke started talking about how she hated her life and how depressed she was etc. I opened my mouth to tell her to shut up, that we all had issues etc and you wouldn't believe what happened. I opened my gob and a bit of Psalm 23 just flew out of it and she burst into tears! Well, having a discerning spirit and all (if I may say so myself), I perceived this was a Holy Spirit moment and held her. I asked if she minded me calling Vanessa and she said it was okay. Vanessa came round and we both prayed for her. As Vanessa hugged Foluke, she spoke softly into her ear, 'In the name of Jesus, you spirit of depression, come out!' Foluke shivered a bit, exhaled through her mouth, turned to us and said with a beatific smile on her face, 'I felt it leave'. She didn't exactly commit her life to Christ, but what a difference it's made already! She called me at work first thing the next day and she sounded so happy. She never sounds happy. She said, 'I don't know what you guys did but when I went to bed there was such a peaceful presence in my room. I fell asleep immediately. That never happens. I'm going to call Vanessa to thank her as well. There might be something in this church thing after all.'

Thank you, Jesus. It's true. True blessing comes when you bless others. Plus I didn't think of Zack all the time I was with Foluke. Not once. That in itself is a miracle. Does that mean I'm healed of him? Helping others is the key. I'll call Pastor Michael and see if there's a community outreach or something I can volunteer for. That'll keep me away from mischief (ie Zack). I will also endeavour to make more church friends, even if church folks normally freak me out. I tend to think they're on a higher spiritual level than me. Well, they look it. Which is why I haven't made any real friends since I started going there. Vanessa says it's because I'm too self-centred. (Like, anyone notices me anyway!) The membership is about 300 so it's kind of hard to spot new people. Pastor Michael is nice though. He knows everyone and is always smiling. His teeth must hurt. Not sure about his wife, though. I get the feeling she would like to be known as someone other than 'the pastor's wife'.

I haven't spoken to Zack in 12 days. I wonder what and how he's doing. Is he okay?

Friday April 26

He thus revealed his glory, and his disciples put their faith in him (John 2:11).

I called Zack this afternoon. I couldn't take it anymore. Called his mobile then hung up when I heard his voice. Of course, I dialled 141 to hide my number, but he knew it was me. He called me back straightaway.

'Kemi, are you okay?'

Put the phone down girl. Hang up! NOW!

'I... I just wanted to find out how you were doing.'

'I'm alright. You?'

'Okay. I've... I've got to go.'

'Kemi, you sound a bit... *confused*. I love you. I really wish I didn't but I do. You might not know what you want, but all I've ever wanted was for you to be happy. Even if all you do is trample on my heart.'

'I'm sorry, Zack. I really am. Bye.'

I just knew he was going to do that. Always got to be a hero. And I do know what I want. I want and have Jesus.

I need deliverance. That's it. I'm going to the prayer meeting tonight. I'm going to cast down everything that exalts itself against the knowledge of Christ in my life. I will be free. The devil shall not reign in my life anymore. That boy should be glad he has someone like me praying for his happiness in the throne room of heaven. I slay demons on his behalf and this is the thanks I get?! Call me *confused?* I'll show him *confused!*

Who am I trying to kid? The Bible's right. Once you sleep with someone, you're bonded with them in such a way that retrieval is only possible via electrocution. I shouldn't have called Zack. Just hearing his voice made me feel weak. If only he would accept Christ. Everything would be perfect. I'm going to the prayer meeting. Need a serious lift of the Jesus kind. Maybe I can get Pastor Michael to lay hands on me. (Er, no, I take that back.)

11.30pm

Another stunner of a meeting. I don't usually like going to prayer meetings because a) they can be rather tiring and b) the noise level tends to be a bit much – and God help us if it's led by a Nigerian. Jesus himself would have to make an appearance if only to tell them to quit their hollering and, no, he's not deaf and could they PLEASE TURN THE NOISE DOWN?

Tonight was alright though. Vanessa rather subdued. Pre-wedding nerves, I think. It's in a month. I hope she's okay.

Invited Foluke (seeing as I'm on a 'help yourself by helping your neighbour' roll) to church but she declined. 'You don't waste any time, do you? I said there might be something in this church thing. I didn't say I was coming. Give a woman a break!!' Just goes to show that salvation is really of the Lord. After all I've done for her, praying and casting out demons (well, I was there in person so theoretically I was involved), you would think she would be grateful. God, how do you put up with us?

I will not call Zack. I am strong. Like a mountain. What was today's verse? Yes, I put my faith in God. He's the only one that can fulfil my needs. Not Zack, not Vanessa, not my pastor – but Jesus. Question: why do I feel this so strongly about Jesus sometimes, and other times I feel like I'm just going through the motions?

I volunteered to go street evangelising tomorrow. In Camden, of all places. I don't know what came over me. It seemed like a good idea at the time. Okay, so I volunteered because I didn't want to stay home feeling sorry for myself, but I'll be saving the world! I just hope I get home in peace and not in pieces. Everyone knows Camden is inhabited by the devil himself. Well, that's what Vanessa says. She's been a

Christian longer than Jesus so she should know.

I hope I don't run into anyone I know. That would be soooo embarrassing.

Saturday April 27

Jesus answered, 'I tell you the truth, no one can enter the kingdom of God unless he is born of water and the Spirit. Flesh gives birth to flesh, but the Spirit gives birth to spirit (John 3:5,6).

5.38pm

What a horrendous day! Why is my life such a drama? All I want to do is get married (to Zack preferably), breed and live out my faith in blissful Technicolor but, no, everything I do has to take on Bridget Jones-like proportions.

This was the plan: meet Vanessa + Pastor Michael + wife + other Sanctifieds at Camden Station. Great! No problem. Turned up but no one was there except the Sanctifieds (read: Boring Super Spirituals). Seeing as I was filled with the power of the Holy Ghost as I prayed this morning (Nigerian style) for a bountiful harvest, I took charge of the situation. 'Right, where should we stand?' They looked at me weirdly until I realised that we hadn't been introduced to each other properly yet so we did that. Then we hung around for a few moments pretending that we weren't praying for the world to end right then and there so we wouldn't have to do this evangelism stuff. I realised we weren't going to get anywhere lurking around like fugitives and told everyone they were welcome to join me in preaching if they wanted to. We crossed the road and stood outside the Barclays Bank opposite the station and I started reading from John's Gospel. One of the Sanctifieds started handing out tracts and we even prayed for some people. Once I got over the fact that a) the earth wasn't going to swallow me, b) my voice wasn't shaking too much and c) Amanda and Robert were actually in the crowd of people, looking very much an item, and looking at me like I was a Martian, I think I did okay, soldiering on like the apostle because I am not ashamed of the gospel of Jesus Christ.

Actually, I was embarrassed that Amanda and Robert saw me but I figured: How bad can life get? Hmm. It got worse. I was rounding off with a call for people to accept Jesus as Lord when I spotted Zack. He of the most perfect guy in the world. He of the 'I really want to live with him in a Technicolor dream life'. And, not to go on or anything, but he of 'I love you even if all you do is trample on my heart'. Yes, he of all these things had his arm around some girl who was looking at him like she wanted to eat him right there and then. When I saw them, my voice faltered. Naturally. But, like an eagle, I picked myself up and carried on with the work of the Lord. I saw him start when he heard my voice, look at me – right at me – and carry on walking. With his arm around the girl, who was nattering like the husband-stealer she was.

He's not your husband.

I don't want to talk about it, Lord. Couldn't you have chosen some other place for him to go to? I just want to be left alone. Is that too much to ask? Why was he in Camden, anyway? He never comes to Camden. He hates it. I bet you it was some Jezebel woman with him. She probably wanted to lend a healing hand (as a friend, of course) to help him get through his difficult time of getting over a Delilah-type person masquerading as a Christian fundamentalist. I could kill her.

I'm sorry, Lord. Is this what I've turned into? A raving lunatic? I probably qualify for a fast track application for the Jezebel club. No questions asked. And to top it off, get this: two of the Sanctifieds got their pockets picked! They were praying individually for two guys and, suddenly, the guys they were praying for started running down the High Street. Needless to say, we called it a day after that.

As for Amanda and Robert, I just hope they know what they're doing. Dating a co-worker is a tricky business. Mind you, a little happiness never hurt anyone.

All in all, an eventful day. Lord, who was the girl with Zack? What were they doing there? Just asking a simple question, Lord. Yes, I do trust you – but a physical appearance now and then wouldn't hurt. I wonder if Vanessa knows the girl Zack was with. Not that she would tell me anything, as I'm not even supposed to be fraternising with him. I hope Vanessa's okay. She never misses street evangelism. I'm sure it's the wedding. There must be so much to do.

Monday May 6

After this, the word of the LORD came to Abram in a vision:
'Do not be afraid Abram. I am your shield, your very great
reward' (Genesis 15:1).

Hello! Long time, no write. I've just been so busy! I got a pay rise. Thank you, Jesus!

After the Camden street evangelism massacre (I mean *blessing* not massacre – I really must learn how to choose my words), I got home and basically had a whinge about everything. Then I had a read through my journal and I couldn't believe what I was reading. I mean, who's that self-centred person in the pages? And that obsession with Zack?! What's that all about?

Vanessa was right. I needed deliverance. I needed to be released from everything that wasn't from the throne room of heaven. So I went on a five-day fast and I tell you, I can FEEL the difference. I feel like a spiritual weapon of satanic destruction and godly blessing. Even Vanessa's noticed. 'You're just full of Bible verses and faith, aren't you?' Of course I am. I am a born again, demon-kicking Christian. Jesus is Lord! Hallelu-yah!

I sauntered into work the Monday after Camden (the first day of my fast), went into Amanda's office and said, 'God bless you, Amanda, and you too, Robert.' (He was sort of lurking behind the door.) 'I hope it works out well for the two of you. Jesus is Lord!' And off I went, full of Holy Ghost goodness. At that precise moment I knew how Jesus felt. I too loved the world so much that I was willing to forfeit five days of food to save humanity from the attack of the self-centred Christian.

By noon I was ravenous.

At 2pm I was faint with hunger.

At 4pm I was desperate.

At 5pm I crawled out of the office and at 6pm I got home and made a heroic dash for the fridge. Inside, there was a note from Mum stuck on a mountain of microwave dishes: *For you to break your fast with. Don't understand what you're doing but we love you anyway. Dad and I are always here for you. We'll talk when you're ready.* My parents have the key to my flat, though they rarely use it. I'm glad they used it this time though. I was starving!

By day three I was back on track, although it was making me slightly sanctimonious. On day five part of me didn't want the fast to end but end it did. And now, I just love everyone and everything, but most especially I love Jesus! And I'm handing out tracts in Camden again this weekend. Hopefully, we'll get some Christ commitments. We all need Jesus. Even Zack, but I know now that he is not my responsibility. He's God's and that's okay with me. Finally.

And my cousin Foluke is still okay. We're going to Smollensky's on Friday. With the Sanctifieds.

I just lurve the world. Even the bus-stop friend's girlfriend. Still wouldn't want to be stuck on the same bus seat with her though. Lurve or not, she's still a nutter.

Wednesday May 8

Therefore, I urge you, brothers, in view of God's mercy, to offer your bodies as living sacrifices, holy and pleasing to God – this is your spiritual act of worship (Romans 12:1).

Lord, make Friday come quickly! Can't wait. It's the first time I've been out properly since I became a Christian. I've been hanging out with the Sanctifieds a bit lately. They're so strong in their faith. I hope I can be more like them. They've never been to Smollensky's so are rather excited. Lord, let Friday come quickly!

Vanessa's wedding is in less than three weeks. I can't wait for that, either. She's been rather subdued lately but I'm sure she'll pick up soon. She's getting married. How bad can life be?

Friday May 10

One man considers one day more sacred than another; another man considers every day alike. Each one should be fully convinced in his own mind (Romans 14:5).

Look at that! The Holy Spirit knows today is Friday. Smollensky day! Bring on the jazz!

Saturday May 11

The ways of the LORD are right; the righteous walk in them, but the rebellious stumble in them (Hosea 14:9).

Today's Camden street blessing went okay. It was just the Sanctifieds and myself. Not that we did much. We handed out tracts for a few minutes, then we went shopping. Much more fun.

Zack was at Smollensky's last night. It was okay actually. He was alone. I introduced him to the Sanctifieds and they all liked him. Like I knew they would. *Everyone* loves Zack. He and Foluke chatted for ages. They've always got on and he was nice to her, even though it's always been clear to everyone she was a lunatic. As we were going, he whispered in my ear, 'She was just a friend'. I pretended I didn't know what he was talking about. Men can be so clueless. It was pretty evident to anyone looking that the woman I saw in Camden had more than friendship on her mind but I didn't think it was my place to say anything.

'He still loves you,' Foluke said when we parted at the station.

'I love the Lord more,' I replied.

Monday May 13

The lions may grow weak and hungry, but those who seek the LORD lack no good thing (Psalm 34:10).

Mum went to hospital for a check-up today so I'm going to see her after work. Cover her with your healing hands, Lord. She's my mother. She might not know you yet, but I do.

Later

Zack just dropped me off home. He was at my parents' when I got there. Like I thought he would be. He's like a son to them. Which is why I cannot tell them to choose between us. It wouldn't be fair. Nor right. Even if it makes things rather complicated for me. I try to avoid him and try even harder not to tell my parents to put a sock in it every time they update me on his life. It's rather tiring, but what am I supposed to do? They think I'll come to my senses and sail into the marital sunset with Zack, but they'll get the message eventually; like when I bring home another man or he tells them he's got a girlfriend. Not that we'll do that for a while yet. We don't want to give them apoplexies.

We had a pleasant ride home actually. We talked about work, church and life.

It was just a ride, Lord. I'm not stupid. My barriers are up. I will not fall. I feel nothing for him. Absolutely nothing.

Sure, I know... pride goes before a fall. I'm not having this conversation. Good night.

Wednesday May 15

Awake and rise to my defence! Contend for me, my God and LORD (Psalm 35:23).

Had a look at the Singing Diapers post-advertising quarterly figures. Sales are fantastic! The consumers are happy, Windy CEO is happy: 'Good stuff, Kemi. Good stuff!' And I'm happy – because moments like these give me a sense of self-righteousness about my job that I wish I had all the time. Thing is, Windy CEO is so happy he wants us/me to handle all their product campaigns from now on. Good news but a lot of work. But I'm up for it. God is truly enlarging my territory. It means my other campaigns will suffer a bit but that's okay. Singing Diapers is hot stuff now and anyway, let's face it... organic water and water-inflated bras? I'm a consumer and I certainly wouldn't buy them.

Had a quick natter with Vanessa on the telephone. We're doing lunch. Hope she's okay. She's getting married in less than two weeks and she looks as miserable as sin (not that she ever sins because she's Jesus' blood sister). After that, I'm zooming off to Leeds for two days for strategic meetings with Smelly et al.

Life's a breeze and I love it!

After lunch

I'm writing this on the train to Leeds. Isn't life strange? I've spent all my (admittedly short) Christian life wishing I was more like Vanessa and she started lunch by telling me how much *she envied me.* I couldn't believe it, nor could I understand it. I've always thought she looked down on me because I wasn't spiritual enough. 'No, Kemi. We don't need spiritual people in the church. We need more people like you because you're real, and less people like me. I'm a preacher's daughter. I accepted the Lord when I was eight years old because that was what was expected of me. I haven't done anything remarkable with my life. I was born in the church, went to church school and now I work in a law firm that specialises in *Christian* ministries. My life revolves around the church and three weeks ago, I came to the conclusion that I didn't want it to be that way any more. I want to live. I want to do stuff I've never done before. I need a change and I need it now.'

She was serious.

'But what about Mark?' I spluttered over my chicken salad wrap.

'I don't know.'

If she didn't know, what hope was there for the rest of us?

'So you're leaving the church?' I asked, visions of her joining a hippy commune in Uttar Pradesh flooding my mind.

'Don't be silly. Of course not! I don't know what I'm going to do yet. Today is my last day at work for a while. I'm taking a sabbatical. I'm going to see my parents after work. The wedding's been postponed. Spoke to Mark last night. He's not happy but I've made up my mind. I know nobody will understand. Sorry.'

'But what about the reception, the wedding dress, the invites… What will people say? What about the money that's been spent?'

She shrugged. 'Kemi, I've thought about other people all my life and always done the right thing. As of this particular season in my life, I just want to do what's right for Vanessa.'

Crikey! You think you know someone and then something like this happens and it's like you're watching *Britain's Most Wanted* (not that I'm voyeuristic enough to watch something like that, being sanctified and all, but one must do one's patriotic duty). You look at the TV screen, blink, look again and realise that, no, you weren't mistaken. The person on the screen is your sister (which is how I regard Vanessa). Not that I'm saying she's a criminal or anything. But Vanessa of all people, *finding* herself? Come back quickly, Jesus! I repent of all my sins!

Sunday May 19

Grace and peace be yours in abundance through the knowledge of God and of Jesus our Lord (2 Peter 1:2).

Back in London. Came back on Friday and went straight to my parents'. I stayed over and on Saturday I was just about to leave when Zack came. He was going to help Dad with the garden. Usually I would run out the door as soon as he appeared at my parents' but I kind of decided that I was being silly. Was I going to run from him forever? He's not the devil incarnate and we have been talking on the phone since we bumped into each other at Smollensky's, so I stayed. It was just like old times: Zack, Mum and Dad, me. It was great. Afterwards, Zack drove me home... and that was when it happened.

I invited him in for coffee. Like, I didn't know what I was doing? He's my weakness and I had no business being anywhere alone with him. Maybe I thought I could handle it, being spiritually supercharged and all. Maybe I thought if I gave in just this once, I could repent afterwards and relocate to Mozambique where no one would ever find me. Maybe it was a combination of these 'maybes'. I don't know.

To be fair, *he* asked *me* if I thought it was a good idea inviting him in.

'Don't be silly,' I said. 'We're both adults.'

He shook his head, got back in the car, turned on the engine, then turned it off. Then he looked at me, his eyes full of questions and I found I had tears in mine – because I knew how the night would end yet felt powerless to do anything about it. He got out of the car and we both went inside.

Today is Sunday and I am not going to church. Zack is still here and we're both trying to live in the present. And I'm trying very hard not to come face to face with the person in the mirror.

I finished putting the breakfast things away when he came up behind me and gave me a hug. I turned round and buried my head in his shoulder. His arms were so strong and so comforting. How could I say no to this? I love having him with me. I love the feel of his arms around me. When he's with me, I feel so safe and so loved. I can't give him up. I *can't*.

My tears spilled onto Zack's neck. I pulled away from him and he kissed me, which made the tears come even harder.

What part has a believer with an unbeliever?

Lord, help me.

'Where do we go from here?' he asked quietly.

'I don't know.' And I didn't. I knew we shouldn't go anywhere but I wanted us to go somewhere.

We spent the rest of the day watching videos. It was easier than talking.

I love Zack and I love being intimate with him. Does God even understand the kind of challenges people like me face in the world? Maybe some people are content to be God's own spouse (and I seriously doubt that – after all, we all have needs), but I'm not. I've been deluding myself all this time. So what if the Bible says sex before marriage is wrong? Why is it wrong? Lots of people have sex before marriage. Does that mean they're cursed for all eternity? They don't look cursed to me. And what if I never find someone to marry? I would be like the Sanctifieds... desperately trying to fill the void with spiritual busyness all the while pretending they aren't lonely. There are only so many conferences, prayer meetings, evangelism outreaches and goodness knows what else that one can be involved in.

My head hurts.

Oh Lord, I hear you loud and clear. I wish I was repentant but I'm not. I wish I could say it wouldn't happen again but I can't – because I know that it *will* happen. Again and again. What kind of Christian am I?

Monday May 20

'Then you will call upon me and come and pray to me, and I will listen to you. You will seek me and find me when you seek me with all your heart. I will be found by you,' declares the LORD *(Jeremiah 29:12-14).*

Great. Just the Bible verse I needed today. Talk about laying on the guilt. I can't talk about this, Lord. It seems pretty straightforward to me. I want Zack and I can't have him because he doesn't believe your Son is the only way to eternal life. I did mention I committed the sin of pre-marital sex, didn't

I? A sin I don't want to repent of because that would mean I was sorry? And I am not.

I need to think.

I need to call Vanessa.

No I don't.

I need a get a grip and think.

Later

Saw Amanda and Robert as I was packing up after work. He actually had his arm around her. Like he didn't care who saw. We all saw and pretended we didn't. Maybe life's too short not to grab some relational happiness. Even if the person does smell like a skunk.

I found myself at Vanessa's after work. I knew Zack was expecting me at his place. But I just couldn't face it. My head is all muddled up. My heart sank when her Dad, Pastor Daniel, opened the front door to let me in. Great! I didn't want him to see my eyes so I mumbled a quick hello and shuffled inside.

'Kemi, come back here and give your uncle a hug! I haven't seen you in weeks!'

I shuffled back, gave him an anorexic hug and ran up to Vanessa's room before he could say anything else. I'll say one thing for the man, though. He sure didn't look like someone whose daughter just cancelled a wedding because she had an identity crisis. I don't think my Mum would be that understanding. Dad, maybe. But not Mum. She can be a bit of a battleaxe sometimes. A beautifully preserved battleaxe, I hasten to add. What would she say if she knew I spent last night with Zack? And the night before? She probably knows already, anyway. I don't know how, but she knows stuff. My friends tell me all mothers are like that. They just *know*.

Vanessa was in bed reading *Woman Alive* magazine. She sat up when I opened her door.

'You slept with him again, didn't you?'

If she knew the answer, why was she asking? I took off my shoes and sat on her bed. My mobile rang. Zack's number flashed up. I didn't want to answer it.

'Answer it,' Vanessa said.

'Don't want to,' I said irritably. A minute later, I got a text from him. CALL ME WHN U LEAVE V'S. I vowed to find another best friend. Everybody always knows where to find me.

'You still haven't answered my question.'

'Everything's changed. I love Zack. I've always loved him. You like him too, don't you. Or has that changed? So he's not a born-again Christian. Big deal. So we had sex before marriage. Is that so bad? Look around you, Vanessa. Loads of people have sex before marriage and they go on to have great marriages. Admit it: you sometimes feel that your faith is more of a noose than a lifeline.'

Vanessa looked at me for a moment. 'You didn't think this way last week.'

I looked away. She wouldn't understand. I got off the bed and put on my shoes just as the bedroom door opened and Vanessa's mother came in.

'Kemi, you silly girl. Come and give me a hug. Are you okay? We were praying for you this morning. Your name was very heavy on our hearts. My dear, you look a bit peaky. Are you sure you're okay?'

'I'm okay,' I said when she let me get a word in. 'Just a bit tired. A lot on at work, you know.' I smiled weakly at Vanessa. 'I guess I'll see you later.'

Vanessa smiled. Rather sadly, I thought. I gave my goodbyes and stood hesitating outside their house. I didn't know what to do next. I didn't want to see Zack. I didn't want to see my parents. I didn't want see Foluke. And I especially did not want to see the Sanctifieds. So I went to the cinema, sat at the back, ate too much chocolate, and cried all the way through the movie.

Faith and sex. The two have no business being together.

Tuesday May 21

Put your hope in God, for I will yet praise him, my Saviour and my God (Psalm 43:5).

I'm at Zack's. I spent the night. I went to his place after the movie, rang the bell and stood on the doorstep bawling my eyes out. I must have looked a sight. Snot was coming out of my nose, my eyes were all red and swollen and I could barely speak. Zack opened the door, saw me standing there, snot and all, took my hand and led me upstairs. Then he ran me a bath and I fell asleep straight after. He called Vanessa while I was in the bath to let her know I hadn't been run over by a bus in my fragile (read: convicted) state.

Zack deserves better. Much better.

'I don't want anyone else but you,' he said when I told him as much. 'Even if you have made me a fool.'

I've made fools of us both.

Wednesday May 22

Yet a time is coming and has now come when the true worshippers will worship the Father in spirit and in truth, for they are the kind of worshippers the Father seeks (John 4:23).

These daily verses. There are days when they're my lifeline and I drink them in like water in the desert and there are days when I can barely stand to read them because I'm afraid of what I'll find.

Today is one of those second sorts of days. Fake worshippers. Yep, I'm one of them.

I've been sleeping with Zack for the last three nights.

Mustn't think about that now.

Robert and Amanda are really going full throttle with their relationship thing. They come into work together and leave together. I really hope it works out for them. I don't think the company can handle two psychotic marketing women in the office (and I am definitely included in this particular psychological count). But what about Robert's smell? Is Amanda nostrilogically challenged or something? Who cares?! They're in love!

I wonder how Zack is doing right now. I know we have to talk but I keep putting it off. Things are rather tense between us. And Vanessa keeps coming at me with Bible verses on being 'unequally yoked' et al. I should shove her Bible down her throat just so she gets a taste of what it's like for people to hear her preach.

Ouch!

Can't believe I actually wrote that.

I hope Zack's okay. He didn't really talk this morning. Just gave me a kiss when we parted at the tube station. Maybe it's because of his caseload. Barristers are perpetually busy, right?

Who am I kidding? He's mad at me. I have to decide: Zack or God. At this present moment, Zack is infinitely more appealing. He's real. I can touch him and feel him (okay, don't go there). I cannot see or touch Jesus. He's up there with the stars.

I wish I was a better Christian. I wish the Bible wasn't so pedantic about certain issues. I wish I could backtrack to last week when I was at one with God the Father, God the Son and God the Holy Ghost.

I'm still here.

Not now, Lord. You just want to steal my joy.

Why do you run from me, beloved?

Lord, just leave me alone. I need to think. To focus.

Later

Mum's just called me at work.

'Are you okay? You haven't called home in three days,' she said.

'Sorry. Work's a bit crazy. How's Dad?'

'Don't change the subject, I'm not stupid. I don't know what's going on between you and Zack but just sort it out, okay? It's getting tedious. Anyway, got to go. I'm going to see Foluke. Love you.'

'Love you, too.'

I tried getting back to work but couldn't concentrate. God. Zack. Love. Sex. My mind's whirling around. I feel vulnerable and exposed. Like something is hovering over me that I can't shake off. It's horrible. Definition of God: the Great Joy Stealer who gives people impossible desires and needs that cannot be met by his archaic rules.

I can't believe I just wrote that. Get a grip, Kemi! So you're sleeping with Zack. Big deal. Life is for the living. Live it to the full, girl!

I'm going to Zack's, pick up my stuff and go to my parents.

No, not my parents. I'll go to my flat. I need to be alone. To think. And pray.

Pray? To whom? And for what? I haven't done anything to be ashamed of. I just wish this cloud hanging over me would go away.

Sunday May 26

I am unworthy – how can I reply to you? I put my hand over my mouth (Job 40:4).

It really hasn't been a good week. Re-reading my last entry just confirmed what everyone but me has always known: I am not of sound mind. I left work early on Wednesday, went to Zack's to get my stuff, and then went back to my flat. I turned off my mobile, yanked the plug off my telephone and just sat in the silent darkened room. I didn't know what else to do. I fell asleep and was woken up by someone beating down my front door. I thought I was being burgled until I heard Zack yelling through the letter flap, 'Kemi Smith, if you're in there, open the door this very minute!' What did he think he was doing, hammering on my front door at 11 at night? What would people think?

'Who cares what they think?!' he said when I let him in and gave him a piece of my mind. 'Don't you think it's about time you thought about other people? You go to my flat, pack up your things and leave. Just like that. No note, no nothing. Your mobile is off and your landline keeps on going to voicemail. I called your office and they told me you left work early. Tell me, Kemi, if you were in my shoes, wouldn't you worry?'

'Sorry. I wasn't thinking. I wanted some time to myself.'

'Well, now you've got it. I've had enough of this. Give me my keys.'

'What?'

'The spare keys to my flat. I want them back. I just came to check you were okay and now that I know you are, I'm going home. With my keys. I've had enough.'

'Zack, please! I just need some time to think... '

'The keys, Kemi!'

I handed over the keys and went to put my arms around him.

He tensed and stepped aside. Then he walked out of my flat. Just like that. I suppose the man could only take so much. Visions of life without him flashed before my eyes and I panicked. I ran after him and pulled at him... his jacket... his arm... anything I could grab, all the while crying and begging him to stay. He pushed me away, got into his car and sped off.

I did this. I did this to him and now he's gone. Not that I blame him. I haven't exactly treated him right. I bet you he's gone to that... that harridan he was hanging around with in Camden. I'll kill her! I'll scratch her eyes out and put her on a pyre specially made for husband-stealers, and dance on it.

Dear Lord, I'm sorry! I didn't mean that.

Yes, I did.

No, I didn't.

I so meant it! I'll kill her if I see her with him. He's mine, not hers! Zack has been a part of my life for seven years. Seven years! And I'm not going to let seven years of history go just like that. No way. Even if I am a demon-kicking, tongue-speaking, hypocritical backslidden Pentecostal. And I don't care what Vanessa says about breaking all ties to anything standing in the way of God's glory. What does she know? She's Jesus' blood sister.

Seven years! I met Zack at uni. We were both in our final year. He was a law scholarship student and I was studying marketing. We started dating two years after. We dated for three and a half years. Then I became a Jesus Freak and the story ended. Well, almost.

Zack's special, and not just because he's an orphan and he's got where he is today by sheer graft. It's not his looks (although everyone knows he was made on a Sunday so God really took his time creating him). It's not that. He's one of the kindest, most compassionate and most resilient people I've ever known in my life. When I'm with him, I feel ten feet tall. When I think of Zack, I think of a brick house: solid and utterly dependable. And the thought of being without this particular brick house is rather frightening. I've been kidding myself this last year. It was never finished between Zack and me. I just liked to pretend it was.

Trust also in me.

God, please, not tonight. I'm hurting. I wish I could give this to you but I can't. I just can't seem to. I created this mess. It's all my fault. '

Beloved, have you forgotten?... God works for the good of those who love him, who have been called according to his purpose.

What I want is what you want me to give up. I can't do that.

My week didn't get better. I ate way too much chocolate. I had a difficult meeting with Smelly, of the Singing Diapers phenomenon.

'Baby Star!' he announced at the meeting with a self-satisfied smirk on his face. I sensed Sharronne, one of my team, looking at me apprehensively and I refused to make eye contact. The girl needed lessons on subtlety.

'That's the next big thing and Singing Diapers will be there when it happens.'

I took a deep breath. 'Baby Star?'

'Yes. Singing Diapers is going to sponsor the very first Baby Star competition in the UK, possibly the world. Imagine the publicity for our products. It's going to be big. Huge. Awesome.' He was smiling like the cat that got the cream.

'Baby Star?' I repeated.

'A nationwide search for the most talented baby in the UK. Age limit capped at 12 months and the winner gets a year's advertising contract with us, free products and a guaranteed entry in the World Baby Star competition. Imagine the impact!'

He clapped his hands and beamed.

'*World* Baby Star?'

'Genius or what? I knew you would like it!'

Sharronne leaned forward. 'But there are hundreds of baby competitions around the country. What makes Baby Star so different?'

'That, Sharon... '

'Sha-rr-onne.'

'... is why you and Kemi are here. You are going to make Baby Star the only baby competition worth entering. Think of the possibilities for Singing Diapers!'

I did the only thing that made sense at that particular time. I called lunch.

'Ideas seem to come quicker on a full stomach,' I said, smiling at the table and nodding at Sharronne.

She got up and directed everyone to the curry puffs and egg mayonnaise sandwiches. I kept on smiling even when Smelly winked at me over his sagging paper plate. Egomaniac! He really does think he has something going on with this Baby Star.

Baby Star. My eyes clouded over. I saw pushy parents, a television studio filled with dirty nappies and screaming babies... and placard-carrying liberals outside in the street campaigning against the abuse and commercialisation of tiny tots.

Baby Star. What are the babies going to be judged on? How well they gurgle, waddle or dribble? Beam me up, Lord!

The idea had to be killed. Immediately.

Fortunately, Smelly was called away after lunch so the meeting couldn't continue. Why did I ever think I could head up this account? The execs have mushrooms for brains! And I, Singing Diapers' marketing executive, am one step away from relocating to Marrakesh.

Oh, yes. Something else happened. Robert doesn't smell anymore! He came into the meeting room earlier when we were setting up the latest figures on Powerpoint, to give someone a message or something. And immediately everyone held their breath – a habit, not to put too fine a point on it, we have been forced to develop. When, needing air, I exhaled... it hit me. There was no smell. Everyone looked at each other and at Robert. He looked at us with a strange expression on his face and went into Amanda's office. I waited a minute then followed him inside. He and Amanda were standing by the window. Holding hands.

'Morning, Kemi. How's the soul-saving?' Amanda asked, but she wasn't really being horrible.

'So-so. Umm... listen... can I have a quick word with you, later?'

'How about now? Robert's just leaving.' And so he was. He gave her a peck on the cheek, nodded at me and left.

I didn't really know how to go on. After all, it was none of my business. But I figured I had to say something. Anything. I cleared my throat.

'Amanda... you and Robert... Are you sure?'

'Nobody is 100 per cent sure about anything. Don't worry, I know what people are saying. I can see it in their eyes when Robert and I walk into the office together. But you know what? I don't care. Life's too short. Robert didn't want anyone knowing our business but I didn't see any reason for hiding. I'm 35 and he's 30. We're both adults. The office will get over it.'

'What about the office rules on colleagues dating?'

She muttered an expletive and looked out of her window, staring blank-eyed at the milling crowds on Oxford Street.

'I've been selling dreams to people for ten years. I think it's about time I had a dream of my own.'

That's the second person in as many weeks that's told me they were finding themselves. We were both silent for a while. I thought about God, Zack, Vanessa, my parents and my life. My parents' dream was to be together, despite the vast distance – otherwise known as the Atlantic – separating them. Vanessa's dream is to just be. And Zack? Well, that's another story. And me, what about my dream? Did I even have one that didn't involve Zack and me getting married and having children?

Amanda turned from the window.

'Kemi, you have your faith. Not that it makes much sense to the rest of us, it's rather out there, but you have something.'

'You can have a faith, too.'

'Nah. I live in the real world.'

'Jesus is real.'

'Thanks, but no thanks. Anyway, about Singing Diapers. It's a big one. Keep up the good work.'

She sat down at her desk.

'By the way... let me tell you about Robert's smell. He's severely allergic to a lot of products – fibres and deodorants included. He only just found out someone who can tailor-make him his very own natural deodorant. This week was the trial run. Shame no one bothered to talk to him about it.'

She turned to her computer and started typing. I went as red as my coffee-coloured self could go and crawled out of her office, my thoughts of connecting with her on a woman-to-woman-spiritual level crushed.

Why hadn't Robert said something?

I haven't been to church for two weeks. No doubt, the Sanctifieds are praying for my sensual heart to be refreshed by the cleansing fire of God's holiness. That's if Vanessa hasn't gathered them for a demon-kicking session on my behalf. Actually, I do hope they have been praying for me. I need all the help I can get. I'm trying hard to be strong but all I can think about is Zack. I miss him. I ache for him and at night all I want is to feel his arms around me. Is he okay? Or is he with that Jezebel woman?

Sometimes I wish I could erase the last six weeks from my memory. Sometimes I wish I was repentant for sleeping with Zack. But I'm not. It's as if that intimacy had reached a core of my being that my faith didn't touch. But sometimes I feel such sorrow for my actions, it's all I can do to hold on. I wish I could've shown Zack the true Christian faith à la lived by Vanessa. I fear that all I've done is turn him against God. How he must hate me and all I say I stand for.

I'm such a failure.

Monday May 27

We must go through many hardships to enter the kingdom of God (Acts 14:22).

Still early. These Bible verses. I wonder who chooses them? It's like they know exactly how you'll feel each day and give you something to prolong your misery. I feel like writing to the organisation that publishes this daily devotional and telling them to put a sock in it.

We must go through many hardships ... Hardships. Yeah, like that's going to get people rushing through the church door. People want life, love and liberty, not hardships.

Therefore, there is now no condemnation for those who are in Christ Jesus. Not from where I'm standing. It's been five days and I haven't seen or spoken to Zack. What is he doing? Where is he? Has he seen my parents? Does he think about me? Questions, questions. GET READY FOR WORK, YOU LOSER!

In toilet. At work

I saw my bus-stop friend on the way to work. He's not looking too good. I just know it's something to do with that Jezebel woman otherwise known as his girlfriend ruining his life.

That's probably what people say about me in relation to Zack.

Hardly slept a wink last night. I was thinking of stuff. Earlier, Vanessa and the Sanctifieds came round. It was quite nice actually. They didn't preach at me or ask me why I had missed church and evangelism. They didn't even ask about Zack. Like I didn't notice! I was really depressed before they came round but they really cheered me up. Don't get me wrong. I wasn't leaping up and down by the time they left, but there's nothing like being surrounded by other people when you're wallowing in self-pity. Puts things in perspective.

One of the Sanctifieds is homeless. She's currently roughing it with another Sanctified. And another Sanctified has a mother in a women's refuge. Listening to them, I couldn't help but be thankful for the many blessings God has heaped on my life. So anyway, we all just chilled out. It was great. As they were leaving, Vanessa gave me the-hug-that-spoke-volumes. She didn't say anything. She didn't have to. The girl amazes me. Why can't I be more like her? You know... be more discerning and less self-centred?

So anyway, there we were on the bus this morning, my bus-stop friend and I. I noticed him looking at me and gave him a cheesy smile. No harm in it, I figured. His girlfriend wasn't there to claw my eyes out. He smiled back and started reading his newspaper.

I've decided. I'm going to the prayer meeting on Friday. The last couple of days have shown me just how lonely life without God can be. The whole Zack business and work situation clouded my judgement, but I've decided: home is where God is. And, instead of lamenting over life without Zack, I should rejoice and thank God for making a way out for me. Zack's gone, and, if I have any iota of common sense, I'll leave him be.

It's a shame though, things ending this way. Who would have thought it? It doesn't mean I won't claw the Camden woman's eyes out if I see her with Zack though. She still doesn't have any business being with him.

So, Lord, this is it. I'm coming back home. To you. I'm going to call Vanessa and talk to her. What else has she got to do with her time, having abandoned her job, impending wedding and being the current spokesperson for Slackers Unlimited and all?

We must go through many hardships to enter the kingdom of God.

How true.

Wednesday May 29

The salvation of the righteous comes from the LORD; he is their stronghold in time of trouble (Psalm 37:39).

Can't really write much as I'm in a hurry. Got meetings with Amanda, Smelly; going to see my parents after work; and I promised Homeless Sanctified to go accommodation hunting with her. (Also after work. Must learn how to schedule my time properly.) Ran into my bus-stop friend again on my way home yesterday. I was reading my Bible, trying to reconnect with God, when he got on and sat next to me. I smiled and carried on reading my Bible. Then he cleared his throat.

'You're always reading that Bible,' he said.

'Well, it helps,' I replied.

He said nothing. I went back to my reading.

Then he came out with, 'Give me a verse, any verse, that sums up why anyone would want to believe in this Bible stuff.' He had a mischievous glint in his eye.

'What about: *it is appointed for men to die once, but after this the judgement.'*

I didn't wait for him to answer as it was my stop. Poor bloke's probably on his way to hurl himself off a cliff now. Not that I blame him. If someone gave me such a depressing verse, I would probably do the same. Sweet Jesus, how do you put up with me? I'm supposed to be light in the world and I've just given a man the keys to perpetual depression. Like he needed to be reminded about his death. Beam me up, Lord.

Thursday May 30

I am sending you grain, new wine and oil, enough to satisfy you fully (Joel 2:19).

The prayer meeting is tomorrow. I'm a bit nervous. Looking at today's verse, I've decided to consecrate myself to the Lord.

'Out with the old, on with the new' type of thing. Summer's just round the corner, after all. Not sure if it will help, but I figure if I want to really go full throttle with this Jesus business, then I must start as I intend to go on.

Zack's okay. Mum told me when I went round there yester-day. I could see she wanted to say more but restrained herself (a first).

'Good,' I said, my heart thumping at the mention of his name.

Does he think about me? Is he eating properly? Does he hate me? Has he found someone else? The questions came thick and fast, but I refused to give in and voice them. I am strong. Like an eagle. I am a demon-kicking, tongue-lashing Pentecostal. I can do all things through Christ who strengthens me.

But I miss Zack. It's like an ache. I miss hearing my name from his lips. I miss his strong, comforting arms... stop it, Kemi! *Stop it!*

I'm an eagle. I can do this.

Sunday June 3

If God is for us, who can be against us? (Romans 8:31).

Nothing and no one can be against me because I'm back in the arms of God where I belong. On Friday, after the prayer meeting, I went to see Pastor Michael. I asked Vanessa to come into his office with me, but she declined.

'I think you need to do this yourself. I'll wait outside.'

Well, when I got into the pastor's office, I just started crying and saying, 'I can't do this Jesus thing by myself. It's too hard!'

Pastor Michael smiled and said, 'Welcome to the club!' It was easy after that. We talked for a very long time. About three hours. And Vanessa waited *all that time!* She was even smiling when I came out. How does she do it? It's because she's a pastor's daughter, I concluded. How else can I explain her abnormal behaviour? Like any *normal* Londoner, if I have to wait more than 60 seconds for a lift or something I demand an apology and a refund. It's the world we live in, I tell myself.

'Have you ever resented being a pastor's daughter?' I asked Vanessa when we got back to my flat. She was spending the night.

'All the time,' she replied.

'Really? But you've never said anything, and I'm your best friend.'

'That's because I didn't want you to know how much I envied you. You're so sure of yourself with your fancy job, lovely coffee-coloured skin, high-powered boyfriend... well, ex-boyfriend... and perfect parents.'

She stopped and laughed self-consciously. 'I'm just a pastor's daughter. Nothing remarkable. You, on the other hand, live out your faith in a very real way, warts and all. I don't have the courage to do that.'

'You're having a laugh aren't you? Have you forgotten? I'm a sexual misfit. And all that stuff about being just a pastor's daughter. You're more than that. You've just waited three hours in an empty corridor for me and not once did you complain. What kind of a person does that?'

Vanessa looked away. 'An idiot.'

'No, a friend and a true Christian. Even if the person in question does get on my nerves.'

We were both quiet for a while but it was nice.

'Vanessa, maybe you shouldn't try so hard? Maybe God just wants you to be.'

'Maybe. Did it help? Pastor Michael, I mean.'

'Yeah. We talked about loads of things. My parents, Zack, you, marriage, sex... everything.'

'What's it like?'

I couldn't believe my ears.

'What's what like?'

'You know... sex.'

'Vanessa, I'm not having this conversation. Have you forgotten who you're speaking to? HELLO! ANYONE THERE?!'

'Don't be so melodramatic. It's just... I've always wondered and if I can't ask you, who can I ask?'

We were both silent again until eventually I spoke.

'It's nice – but the Bible is right. Some people say they can do it and not think twice about it but that's a lie. Because when you sleep with someone, your body, soul and spirit makes a connection with that person and it's like you're bonded... or... well, branded with their spirit or something. Oh, I don't know. But that's the best way I can explain it.'

'Is it true that only women have this connection and men don't?'

'I don't believe that for a minute because sex is so... intimate. Even if a man doesn't feel he's connecting spiritually with everyone he sleeps with, he leaves a little part of the real him with the other person each time they have sex. Well, that's what I think, anyway. What I have problems with is the spiritual and physical consequences part. I mean, I'm not spiritually wired like the people in church. I have needs and I don't think it's fair for God to give me these desires and expect me to sit back and indulge in them *only* when I'm married. The way the church is going, I'll still be unmarried – not to mention sexless – at the second coming.'

It was a depressing thought: a life alone.

'What if I'm bad at it... you know... sex?' Vanessa's voice was pensive.

'What if Mark's bad at it?'

We burst out laughing. Then I thought of Zack and my face clouded over.

'Mark will be okay,' Vanessa said.

Went to church today. I won't lie. It's good to be back. How could I have stayed away so long? When I looked around the church I saw 300 people, each with their own battles and challenges, each believing and trusting in God *in spite* of the challenges. As the choir sang Amazing Grace, I was filled with a wonderful sense of well-being. Suddenly, I really knew that it didn't matter what I did or said: God would always love me. Unconditionally. And nothing I did would ever change that. Even my fixation with Zack. I don't know why I missed it before. I thought back over the last couple of months to the times when I've been so low I thought I couldn't go lower and God would put some Bible verses in my mind to comfort me and steady me when I thought I would fall. I also thought of the gazillion times he would try to lead me in the right direction, only for me to push him away because I wanted to follow my own path. I began to weep. How could I have ever doubted his love and commitment to me?

I went home after the service and read Psalm 23 over and over and over again. Then I read Ephesians 3 about 50 times before falling asleep. Then Foluke woke me up by hollering through my letter box, 'Open the door, you Jesus Freak!' A normal person would simply ring the doorbell. But not Foluke. (I wouldn't change her for the world, though.)

Monday June 4

I write to you, dear children, because your sins have been forgiven on account of his name (1 John 2:12).

Full throttle. That's the best way to describe my day. Full throttle. Smelly has called me 50 times today to find out the latest development on the Singing Diapers Star Baby phenomenon. And Amanda? Well, she walked in today flashing a ring on The Finger. Yes, That Finger. And Robert? He came up to me and said, 'You know, if you hadn't gone to Paris and taken on the Singing Diapers account, Amanda and I would never have got together.'

Taken on. The cheek of it. It was dumped on me! I smiled sweetly and proclaimed God's blessings on their union. They've only known each other five minutes and now they're off to the altar? At least Zack and I had seven years of history, although why I am bringing that up, I'll never know, because that part of my life is SO OVER. I am happy for them. Truly, I am. I just hope they know what they're doing.

And then I found out we'd lost the organic water account and got an earful from Amanda. Apparently the client didn't think I was giving their account the attention it deserved. Yeah, right! The product isn't selling because it's a stupid product. You would think they would at least be creative with their reasons. The way Amanda was carrying on, you would think she didn't know why the client went elsewhere. But that's okay. I'm a demon-kicking, tongue-lashing Pentecostal – a Pentecostal Nigerian no less. I can take it because I'm an eagle soaring high in the sky.

Hmm… I'm also an eagle with a very high probability of losing another major client such as Singing Diapers if I don't come up with valid reasons to terminate Star Baby or World Star Baby or any kind of advertising campaign that has Star and Baby in it. If only God would neutralise Smelly or something. It would make my life so much easier.

The most pleasurable part of my day was having lunch with Dad. I had a right whinge about my stinking job and he told me to give it up.

'But I can't just give up! What else am I supposed to do? I've never done anything else!'

'Then, stop complaining and get on with it. I didn't raise a quitter and you're beginning to sound like one.'

And people think being an only child is all bliss.

I mumbled something in reply. I just wanted some sympathy from my father. Was that too much to ask?

Dad reached over the table and covered my hand with his. 'How are you doing? Really?'

I knew what he was talking about.

'Okay,' I mumbled.

'Good. Now you run off to work and show them what you're made of. I love you.'

'Love you, too. Even if you didn't give me any siblings.'

'I was only thinking of you. This way, you wouldn't have to share your inheritance with anyone.'

We smiled at each other. It was our favourite joke. Mum hates it.

Anyway, I got back to work to find the place in uproar. Smelly, it seems, isn't entirely convinced of my commitment to Singing Diapers and has threatened to move the account to the competition. Got an absolute roasting from Amanda (yes, another one) and spent the rest of the day trying to track down my number one fan: Windy CEO.

I finally got him on his mobile, at Gatwick about to be en route for Malaysia and all points easterly. He said he would speak to me on getting back to London, a week away. I don't like it when clients fob me off. It usually spells disaster. Windy CEO has always been my biggest fan. Have I been usurped? The thought didn't bear thinking about. I am surrounded by slippery enemies, Lord. Not forgetting that Jezebel woman who's probably right now comforting Zack in his hour of need. Get a grip, Kemi. You're such a drama queen!

Thursday June 7

The LORD will make you the head, not the tail. If you pay attention to the commands of the LORD your God that I give you this day and carefully follow them, you will always be at the top, never at the bottom (Deuteronomy 28:13).

Sharronne... friend or foe? Who knows at this point? I saw her getting all chummy with Amanda yesterday, oohing and aahing over her ring and having conversations with Robert in the corridor. A week ago, she wouldn't even go near him, much less touch him, and now it's like they're best friends. And why is she giving me attitude all of a sudden? I feel like a lamb being led to the slaughter. Does Sharronne know something I don't? Strengthen me, Lord. I feel so vulnerable.

I'm the head and not the tail. The head and not the tail. The top and not at the bottom. I wish Zack was here. Whoa! Where did that come from? I'm the head and not the tail. The top, never the bottom. Aargh! I'm going to call Pastor Michael.

30 minutes later

Feeling much, much better. Nothing like a barrel load of God's love to sort you out when you're feeling down. Pastor Michael prayed with me and told me to relinquish my fears to God. I did. Now, if I could just get hold of Sharronne to wring her neck...

Much later

No one would believe the rest of my day. First, I found out that Smelly organised a 'last ditch' meeting to discuss Singing Diapers and Star Baby. With Sharronne. Without checking with me. No wonder Sharronne had been smiling at me like butter wouldn't melt in her mouth.

After that I phoned Vanessa, then Pastor Michael, then my Dad. And then I chewed Sharronne's head off. Told her she was being insubordinate. That I didn't appreciate her arranging meetings with Smelly without my consent, and if she had a problem taking orders from me and working on the Singing Diapers account with me, I would HAPPILY move her to another account. She apologised and said she didn't realise she came across as being insubordinate, that she thought she was taking initiative seeing as I (can you believe the cheek of it?) was having problems holding onto clients' accounts. And anyway, weren't we friends and all?

She must think I was born yesterday. The sly fox. I moved her to the water bra account and brought someone else in, James. A bit of a Rottweiler but at least he's loyal and trustworthy. So now, the whole office thinks I'm a paranoid religious fundamentalist who can't hold onto her clients' accounts. Windy CEO's still not taking my calls. I'm going to Smelly's meeting next Wednesday in Leeds, sans Sharronne. We'll see how that goes seeing as Windy CEO will be there. If I'm still in this job this time next week, it'll be a miracle.

Left work at 9pm. Got home absolutely shattered. Can't wait for the prayer meeting tomorrow. I need a Jesus lift and some affirmation. Dear God, you don't think I over-reacted a bit today, do you?

Saturday June 9

Many are saying of me, 'God will not deliver him.' But you are a shield around me, O LORD; you bestow glory on me and lift up my head (Psalm 3:2,3).

Didn't make it to the prayer meeting yesterday. Had another eventful (read: horrible) day at the office, got home intending to nap for an hour before going to the prayer meeting and somehow slept right through to this morning. What a nightmare week. Just had a call from one of the Sanctifieds. Would I like to go evangelising with them in Camden this afternoon? I looked around my flat and decided a day out was better than looking at the four walls. Even a day in Camden, the devil's lair.

Later

Zack wasn't in Camden. Not that I was looking out for him or anything. As usual most people just walked by as if we didn't exist, but we did have a few people ask us interesting questions. Someone asked me why I was wearing make-up and trendy clothes if I was a Christian. Weren't we supposed to not draw attention to ourselves, to be, you know, plain? I told her that God looked at a person's heart, not at the outward appearance. She seemed dead impressed.

Someone asked why we believed Jesus was alive but Elvis was dead. I told the woman Jesus was/is God and that he came to earth in human form to save people from their sins. By dying and rising from the dead, he defeated death and sin. I also explained that his resurrection was the foundation of the Christian faith. This time it was me that was dead impressed. Didn't know I even knew all this stuff. 'But Elvis is alive,' the woman said. I moved away. Swiftly.

A man asked me if I believed in ghosts. 'My sister speaks to me every night. We were very close. She died a year ago.' My heart broke as I looked at the man. He was only in his early twenties and clearly well acquainted with grief. Pain was oozing out of his pores. One of the Sanctifieds distracted me with a question and, when I turned round again, he was gone.

Rather subdued when I got home. I kept on thinking of the guy and his dead sister. Suddenly a weighty, heavy feeling came upon me and I started crying uncontrollably. In my mind's eye, I could see the guy sitting on his bed talking to someone. Only I couldn't see who he was talking to. I knew that I had to get him to stop talking to whoever it was. There was a sense of urgency about the whole thing that I couldn't explain. I had to get him to stop talking. Immediately. All I could do was weep and speak in a heavenly language. After a while, in my mind's eye, I saw the guy look at his sister's picture by his bed. Then he kept on saying, 'Oh God! Oh God! Help me, I can't take this anymore… ' My mind went blank. Then I heard three words, spoken ever so gently: *It is finished.*

Sunday June 10

He replied, 'Every plant that my heavenly Father has not planted will be pulled by the roots' (Matthew 15:13).

Couldn't wait to get to church. Hardly slept a wink last night. I kept on thinking about what happened to me when I came back from Camden. I didn't know what to call it. An intercessory vision? I couldn't believe it happened to me. I thought that kind of stuff only happened to Triple S People. Does that mean God thought I was super-spiritual? Is it going to be the norm? And what about the man in the 'vision'? Will I ever run into him again? Sometimes there's a lot with God that doesn't make sense.

Anyway, sprang out of bed at the crack of dawn, showered and was ready by 7.30. The service started at 10. Didn't know what else to do so I went for a neighbourhood prayer walk – a first for me. Back at my flat at 7.45am. Then I did what I really wanted to do. I prayed for direction regarding my job and, most importantly, prayed for Zack. Not passionately or anything. I just prayed that he would receive God's best and nothing else for his life and that was it really. Then, I went to church trying hard not to think about the week ahead with Sharronne, Windy CEO, Smelly and the rest of the *Let's Hate Kemi Collective.*

The service was something else. Awesome doesn't even begin to describe it. Pastor Michael talked about pain. He said we should stop trying to run away from our painful experiences and embrace them instead. He talked about different people from the Bible and from history like Paul, Livingstone and William Wilberforce. He said, 'Did you know that all these people had gone through what often seemed like spectacular failure and pain only to emerge from those experiences fully formed in character as well as in strength?' He then talked about Jesus, how in the Garden of Gethsemane he sweated blood while he thought about the shame, humiliation and pain ahead of him at the cross. But most of all, he thought about the pain of separation from his Father, from whom he had never been separated. Pastor Michael went on about how Jesus thought about you and me before going to that cross, how he chose to walk through the pain because he had something to die for: our sins and our salvation.

The crunch bit was coming. Pastor Michael went on to talk about how the Bible says that God will never give us more pain or whatever than we can bear and that he'll walk through the fire with us. And he asked people – us – if we were carrying our troubles by ourselves or letting the God who loves us carry them for us.

Wow! As he was preaching, the church was filled with such a tender presence of God. Practically everyone started weeping.

Not horribly or anything... but, like, tears of joy and release. It was really moving. It's times like this that I know as surely as I know that the sky is blue that God the Father, God the Son and God the Holy Ghost are real.

Spent some time with Vanessa and Mark after the service. Decided not to tell Vanessa about last night. It's too sacred and, besides, I quite like the idea of sharing secrets with the Lord.

Mark's really good with Vanessa. If only she would relax. Thing is, Mark is so laid back, he's horizontal. Lord, please don't give me someone like him. We wouldn't last a week. I need someone with a bit more fire (read: oomph) in him.

I miss being a couple though. It's been almost three weeks since Zack walked out on me... not that I'm counting or anything or even thinking about him because I am SO focused on the Lord at the moment.

Debated whether to go to my parents or not. Decided not to. Zack will be there and the Bible says we should run from temptation or anything else that's likely to lead us to sin. Zack is not the devil incarnate but maybe I should start treating him like one. If I had done that before, I wouldn't be sitting here inundated with images from LIFE AS A COUPLE.

Trying not to think about the final showdown with Windy CEO coming up this week. Steady my nerves, Lord. I know today's Bible verse talks about being pulled from the roots but it's something I would rather not go through. I don't like pain of any kind. I heard what the pastor said about embracing my pain but I'm not strong like that, Lord. I'm not. If you could just neutralise Smelly and charm Windy CEO or something so that he'll agree to everything I say, life would be one perfect pain-free peach.

Tuesday June 12

LORD, who may dwell in your sanctuary? Who may live on your holy hill? (Psalm 15:1).

Tomorrow's the day of reckoning with Smelly and Windy CEO. Amanda and Robert keep looking at me and whispering (or am I imagining it?). Sharronne brushed past me in the corridor without talking to me and everyone in the office keeps on giving me weird looks. I guess it's confirmed then; I'm getting the sack.

The atmosphere in the office is horrible. I'm going out for a breather. Or perhaps I'll just go home. If the decision has been made to sack me, I figure it won't make much difference if I leave work two hours after coming in. God, I'm so weak. Wasn't it only yesterday I was shedding tears of joy in church as your presence filled the hall? I wish I was strong, like Vanessa. I wish I was strong like the Sanctifieds. I wish... I wish... I was a better and stronger Christian.

Later

Grabbed my Bible when I got home and started reading for dear life. I am like Peter in Matthews 14. In the midst of a storm, instead of focusing on Jesus, I get sidetracked and start screaming blue murder when things go haywire. Is it any wonder I mess up? God, how do you put up with me?

I'm going to see my parents. Haven't been for some time now and I miss them. Even Mum – NASA radar not withstanding. She's still the greatest and the bestest. Besides, anything's better than being in my lonely flat wishing tomorrow was over and done with.

Still later

Glad I went. Came back with food packages. Dad's a bit of culinary freak. He's always trying new dishes and driving Mum mad. Today, it was Japanese. Mum refused to eat it, so now she took over the kitchen after him and made my favourite – her yummy shepherd's pie.

'Mum, you've been married for 30 years. Shouldn't you be used to his madcap cooking by now?'

'I gave birth to you. Doesn't mean I don't want to throttle your neck sometimes.'

I told them about the meeting tomorrow and what's been happening at work.

'It'll all work out in the end, you'll see,' Dad said.

Zack wasn't mentioned even though I knew one of the packages Mum set aside was for him. I wish he would just disappear from my life *and* my parents' lives so I could move on properly.

Tomorrow: the day of reckoning. No, strike that. Tomorrow: the day of victory.

Monday June 18

... the fruit of the Spirit is love, joy, peace, patience, kindness, goodness, faithfulness, gentleness and self-control. Against such things there is no law (Galatians 5:22,23).

Do I serve a miracle-working God or what? What a week! What a glorious, glorious, glor-i-ous miraculous week!

Fact: Went to Leeds for meeting with Windy CEO and Smelly. Amanda joined us via conference phone.

Fact: Smelly wanted me out.

Fact: Windy CEO wanted me to stay put.

Fact: Amanda said this about me, 'I think it's safe to say that, without Kemi, Singing Diapers would not be the success it is today. Her campaign and marketing savvy has contributed to a phenomenal increase in sales for your product. You know that as well as I do. And I would go further – to say that we are not willing to pursue a relationship with Singing Diapers without Kemi. So either Andrew (Smelly's real name) goes or we go. And that means taking Kemi with us.'

Fact: I almost fell off my minimalist chair when Amanda finished talking!

Fact: Smelly was moved off Singing Diapers.

Fact: Star Baby is here to stay.

Guess you can't have it all... but what a testimony!

And there's more! I got back to London on Friday and was summoned to Amanda's office. She looked at me briefly, then said, 'Just to let you know, I've recommended you for the Marketing Director post.'

I couldn't believe it. I didn't even know there was such a vacancy. Thank you Jesus!!!!! And they say there is no God. Devil, you are a liar!!!!!

Life is great and I'm just loving it!! I'm going to get my nails done after work and then go and see my parents. I'll probably spend the night. Haven't done that in a while. Hey, maybe I should even call Vanessa and invite her round. I don't think the 'finding herself' quest is working out too good, even though she wouldn't admit it. Finding oneself in London is never a good idea. For starters, the weather stinks. It's mid June and it's raining cats and dogs. It's just depressing. Maybe she should've gone to Uttar Pradesh.

Haven't seen my bus-stop friend and his girlfriend for quite a while either. I hope he's okay... Bible verses about judgement notwithstanding.

Later

Zack was at my parents'. I'm really being tested here. Seems like he's everywhere I go. Why? Anyway, I spent most of the time upstairs in my old room, pretending to look for something. As I started down the stairs, I heard the living room door open and there he was at the foot of the stairs. I won't lie... my heart leapt within me. He's beautiful. How could God create someone like him and not expect him to be idolised? All I wanted to do was just drink him in. So there we were. Me, at the top of the stairs and him, at the bottom, both looking at each other and knowing that, come what may, the story wasn't finished between us. I'm a fool. I've been kidding myself all along.

I'm home and I've got my Bible in my hand. I can sense the tugging of the Holy Spirit on my heart. I can hear Vanessa pleading, 'Kemi, think about what you're doing. Wasn't it only three weeks ago you consecrated yourself to the Lord? Look how far you've come in three weeks. Your victory at work, impending promotion, your strengthened spiritual life. Please, think.'

I can hear Pastor Michael, 'Kemi, keep your eyes on Jesus, the author and finisher of your faith.'

The Sanctifieds: 'Delight yourself in the Lord and he will give you the desires of your heart.'

My parents: 'All we've ever wanted is for you to be happy.'

Foluke: 'Life is too short and too full of pain. Grab some joy while you can.'

Many voices. One decision. I love Zack and I love the Lord. I love being intimate with Zack and I love the personal relationship I have with Jesus. Why can't I have both? I'm not a bad person and I won't let anyone make me feel like I am.

Wednesday June 20

Don't you know that when you offer yourselves to someone to obey him as slaves, you are slaves to the one whom you obey – whether you are slaves to sin, which leads to death, or to obedience, which leads to righteousness? (Romans 6:16).

Don't try and pin that one on me, Lord. I am not a slave to sin. I am not a bad person. Zack is not the devil incarnate. I'm still a tongue-lashing, demon-kicking Pentecostal. Nothing has changed.

Friday June 22

I am not ashamed of the gospel, because it is the power of God for the salvation of everyone who believes... as it is written: 'The righteous will live by faith' (Romans 1:16,17).

At Zack's. I went to his office after work. When he saw me waiting outside, he took my hand in his and we went to his flat. We didn't say anything on the way but I snuggled up close to him all through the journey on the underground. The first time I buried my face in his neck and smelled his aftershave, I thought to myself: *I'm home.* Zack put his arms around me and I held him tighter. At that moment, I didn't want to be anywhere else in the world.

Saturday June 23

Does not wisdom call out? Does not understanding raise her voice? (Proverbs 8:1).

Still at Zack's. This morning, I woke up in his arms. God, I've missed him, I've missed *this*. Being a part of something, someone. When he opened his eyes, the first thing he did was pull me closer to him and kiss the back of my neck. Then he went back to sleep. I watched him sleep for a while before falling asleep again myself.

I will not feel guilty. I am not hurting anyone. I am not a bad person. I will not think of the Lord. I've made my decision, my choice. This is where I want to be.

Sunday June 24

A man's ways seems right to him, but the LORD weighs the heart (Proverbs 21:2).

Church day. I woke up and got ready to go. Zack watched me, his expression kind of hooded.

'I'll be back soon,' I said, before kissing him good-bye. I slipped into the service just after the sermon started and slipped out before Pastor Michael finished. Then I raced back to Zack's. When I rang the doorbell for him to let me in, he opened the door, stood aside, then followed me up the stairs, his eyes boring into my back. When we got upstairs to his flat, he left me and went inside the bedroom, slamming the door behind him. He came out half an hour later while I was in the kitchen and said, 'Vanessa called me after you left.' Then, after a pause, 'I didn't force you to come here.'

'I know,' I said.

'We've been walking up and down this road too long and it's about time we turned a corner.'

'I know. I came back today, didn't I?'

'And tomorrow? Where will you be tomorrow and the day after and the day after that?'

'Where do you want me to be?'

He didn't answer. I decided it was time for me to set it all in stone.

'Zack, I'll be wherever you are,' I said, my heart pounding. I can do this. I'm still an eagle soaring high in the sky.

He still didn't answer. He looked out of the window. Then, 'I would marry you right now, right this very minute if you said yes.'

Oh, Jesus. What have I done? I cannot marry Zack. He doesn't share my faith.

'I didn't think you would answer,' he said, when I stayed quiet. 'Kemi, why are you here?'

'Because... because... I want to be with you.'

Why was he making it so complicated? Can't he see we can make it work? I know we can. Zack turned away from the window and left me standing alone in the kitchen.

Help me, Lord. What should I do? He's hurting so bad. And I'm hurting as well. That marriage proposal? Why did he go and do that?

A few hours later

Still at Zack's. He's in the bedroom and I'm in the living room. I don't want to leave and I don't want to stay either. I wish there was someone I could talk to. No, not Vanessa. She's been calling me all day on my mobile. I've turned it off now so she can't call me. Hah! That'll teach her! She had no right to call Zack. No right at all. Who does she think she is? I'm not like her and I wish she would stop trying to mould me in her image. It's alright for her. She has Mark, but what about me? The chances of me meeting a committed Christian male in church are about as likely as me winning the lottery, which is zilch because I don't play.

As for all that stuff about the spiritual consequences of sex before marriage – does anyone even believe in that stuff anymore? Pur-leese! I need Jesus and I want Zack. I love Jesus and I love Zack. So I've chosen both. Period. If anyone has a problem with it, too bad.

Zack's marriage proposal. Does that mean he'll dump me for kind of turning him down? The thought doesn't bear thinking about.

Later still

My parents just phoned. I saw the number on caller ID. Zack picked up the phone in the bedroom. I could hear him speaking to them about Sunday lunch. You would think a grown man of 28 had the right to have his Sundays to himself, but evidently not. I feel like telling my parents to back off.

Afterwards, Zack came into the living room with his jacket on.

'I'm going out,' he said and walked out of the flat. I knew he was going to my parents for a late lunch. I didn't know what to do but I knew I couldn't leave. If I left, I knew Zack would never let me come back. I had no choice. I had to stay. So I waited for him. He came back about nine.

'I'm glad you stayed,' he said.

Monday June 25

Hear the word of the LORD, you who tremble at his word (Isaiah 66:5).

Bounded into work FULL of energy. What a great day! What a fantastic week this is going to be. I can just feel it. The sun's out, Zack and I are back together, I'm in line for a promotion and everyone at work thinks I'm a star. Thank you, Jesus! Who says you can't have it all?

A lot can happen in a week in advertising. Can you believe that Sharronne? She came into my office all smiley and stuff.

'Just wanted to say well done on the Singing Diapers coup. Shame you're still stuck with Star Baby though.'

Not even Jezebel could ruin my morning, my week or my life. I was on top of the world. I waved my hand airily and replied, 'These things happen.'

Sharronne smiled like a feline and left my office. Vanessa called me. I asked her to meet me in Starbucks for a quick coffee. I knew what she was going to talk about but I didn't care. I also had lots to talk about. All in all, it would be a conversation between two talkative people.

Vanessa didn't waste time. As soon as we sat down with our lattes, she went right into it.

'Kemi, what are you doing?'

'I know what you're going to say but I'm not listening. You don't understand. You never did. I'm not like you. And you had no right to call Zack and tell him whatever you told him.'

'I didn't tell him anything. I just voiced my concern, that's all. You've been here before. Kemi, if you don't think about anything else, think about Zack. It's not fair on him.'

What did she know, being Jesus' blood sister and all? It was easy for her to sit there and tell me how I should be living my life but, down here on earth, things were not that easy.

'Leave Zack out of this.'

'Kemi, I'm your friend, your sister. Talk to me. I might not understand, but I'll try. I know you think that being a pastor's daughter sometimes clouds my ability to live in the real world but I really want to understand.'

'You wouldn't.'

We sipped our coffee in silence for a few minutes.

'Vanessa, it's not just about sex.' I struggled to find the right words. 'It's... it's the whole thing. Church terrifies me sometimes, do you know that? I go in there and I see single middle-aged people with no prospects of settling down with someone and people telling me I'm "single and whole". Or they say, "Maybe God is trying to teach you something before sending you a partner." Or, even worse, that I should focus my attention on serving the Lord instead of focusing on marriage. Well, I'm not going to let anyone steal my desire to be with someone... or rather not just anyone, but Zack. Is that so wrong? Do you think I don't notice that people treat married couples like they're better than singles or something? Well, I'm not having it. Not anymore.'

'You've never said anything about all this before.'

'Vanessa, I'm an only child. If I got to be middle-aged and single, I wouldn't even have little nieces and nephews to play with, to take away the loneliness. And don't tell me God can fulfil all my needs – because that's just lame.'

I looked at my watch. Time to go.

'Can we pray before you go?'

Dear Vanessa. Ever so kind. I felt wretched. It wasn't her fault, though she was probably blaming herself for not being there for me.

'Sure, but hurry,' I said.

She took my hands in hers and said the shortest prayer I'd ever heard her pray: 'Holy Spirit, surround Kemi with your love and presence today, in Jesus' name. Amen.'

I got up. 'Sorry, must dash!'

'Will you be at the prayer meeting on Friday?'

'Maybe. Gotta go. Bye.'

I looked back at our table when I got to the door. Vanessa was still sitting there, staring into space. No doubt wondering how she'll cast the demon out of me in her prayer time. Not that I cared. This is my life and I just want to enjoy it instead of feeling guilty for wanting something so bad.

And what about me, beloved?

I just want to be happy. To be with Zack *and* to be with you. Why do I have to choose?

I went back to work, feeling rather subdued. Was I making a mistake? I stood for a while in the lift lobby thinking about it all. You created Zack, Lord. You know he's not a bad person. Lord, I wish I could explain, make you understand, make you see things from my point of view but I can't because I know you have standards and I've broken your standard for purity.

Back at my desk my phone buzzed. I had a text message. From Vanessa. *Think abt wot u r doing. Please. Going home, will pray for u. Lv u v much. xxxx*

Tuesday June 26

These people come near to me with their mouth and honour me with their lips, but their hearts are far from me (Isaiah 29:13).

These daily Bible verses. I wish they didn't fill me with such dread. Steady me, Lord.

Zack's beginning to withdraw from me again. I know he thinks I'm going to up and leave just like before. I don't know how to convince him I'm in this for the long haul. We haven't told my parents we're back together. I'm waiting for Zack to do it. If I tell Mum, I just know she'll give me a lecture on always putting the other person first in a relationship and I don't think I can bear it.

The bus went past my bus-stop friend this morning. I was on the bus. He was walking and seemed deep in thought. At least he's alive and well. I had visions of him hurling himself off a cliff because of *that* Bible verse.

Things are kind of settled at work. Sharronne still shoots me dirty looks but that's her problem. I can't believe I actually thought we were friends... okay, friendly colleagues. She's evil. Amanda hasn't said anything about my promotion. The vacancy hasn't even been announced yet so I can't really talk about it to anyone. Every time I walk past the Marketing Director's office, I kind of smirk to myself. Yeah, baby! The name on that door will soon be mine.

Singing Diapers is still taxing my brain on the Star Baby front. If I could just find another way of promoting the product, everything would be plain sailing.

All in all, life's a peach. Or close to it.

I raced to Zack's office at lunchtime. It's two stops on the tube. The receptionist, Helen, waved me in. She's mixed race like me. I think that's why she gives this little knowing smile every time she sees me. I wonder if Zack finds her attractive? *Stop it, Kemi!* What is wrong with me? Why do I think every woman is after Zack?

Because I'm terrified he's going to leave me.

He was escorting a client out of his office when I got there. When he saw me, he smiled and gestured to me to come in. He sat me in a chair and sat on the end of the desk looking at me.

'Zack, I meant it when I said I wasn't going anywhere,' I said.

'You know, there are worse things in life than marrying me.'

This wasn't what I expecting. I went there to reassure him of my commitment and dedication. But no, he had to complicate matters. I didn't know how to answer. Besides, I had to race back to my office. Last week's victory notwithstanding, the vultures at work would regroup if I didn't sort out the Singing Diapers campaign. I wanted to touch and hold him, tell him I was for real, but couldn't. I was afraid he would recoil.

'I'll see you later,' I said. He just sat there watching me. What do I have to do to show him I am serious about us?

Friday June 29

So whether you eat or drink or whatever you do, do it all for the glory of God (1 Corinthians 10:31).

Prayer meeting day. And I was planning on going. Even if I feel like everyone there will be talking behind my back. I know I'm not living as a Christian but my heart is in the right place. I refuse to feel condemned.

I told Zack I was spending tonight at my flat and he said, 'I know it's your prayer meeting night. I wouldn't dream of stopping you. Say hi to Vanessa for me.'

I changed my mind about going to the prayer meeting after that. Only I didn't want to spend the night at my flat anymore. I would scream with frustration at the walls closing in on me. And besides, if I was alone, I would feel guilty about my decision to stay with Zack, and I refuse to let that happen.

Foluke's invited us to dinner tomorrow. God help us! Everyone from my dad's side of the family has delusions of culinary grandeur. I've told Foluke this a million times but she doesn't listen. I'm looking forward to the evening though. It will be our first dinner as a couple since getting back together. Even if Foluke is nuts.

Saturday June 30

This is what the LORD has commanded you to do, so that the glory of the LORD may appear to you (Leviticus 9:6).

As expected, Foluke's culinary creation was a disaster. The food was either burnt or not cooked properly. It was hard to determine. Foluke said it was Fijian. Correction, it was meant to be Fijian. We eventually ordered a Malaysian takeaway – but we had a great time.

'I'm glad you guys are back together. You make a lovely couple and life's too short. We all need love.'

I murmured my thanks. Zack looked away. He still didn't trust me not to trample on his heart.

Sunday July 1

And God blessed the seventh day and made it holy, because on it he rested from all the work of creating that he had done (Genesis 2:3).

Sunday. Church day. I sneaked out of bed and got ready to go.

I don't know why I bothered because Zack was awake anyway.

'You know I don't mind you going to church. You're the one that feels the need to hide where you're going.'

I sat on the edge of the bed. 'You could come with me.'

'I would rather not. I don't think I'm Vanessa's favourite person at the moment. Besides, I don't want to embarrass you. Everyone knows you've chosen a heathen over your Lord.'

He was right. I sighed.

'We can do this, Zack.'

He gave me a self-deprecating smile. 'Of course we can. Go on. Go to church. Don't forget we're having lunch at your parents.' He leaned over and gave me a quick kiss on the cheek. 'And say a little prayer for me.'

Once again, I slipped inside near the beginning of the sermon and sat at the back. The service was okay, I guess. I could see Pastor Michael looking at me. I've missed my last two counselling sessions with him. I wondered if Vanessa has told him about Zack. She wouldn't, I decided. I suddenly had another thought: what if Vanessa's told her parents about Zack and me? The thought didn't bear thinking about. I loved Vanessa's parents. They were like mine. I couldn't bear it if they thought badly of me.

The sermon was on God separating the chaff from the wheat or some such thing. I couldn't bear it. I had to leave. I left after about 20 minutes and went to a café that's close by. I ordered an espresso and sat for a while, thinking about everything and nothing. When I saw people spilling out of the church, I hurried out and went back to Zack's.

We had a nice time at my parents'. Mum cornered me in the kitchen when we were tidying up after lunch.

'Is this what you want?' she asked, nodding her head in the direction of Zack in the living room.

'I think so. Yes, it's absolutely what I want.'

'You're my daughter and I love you but Zack... '

'Why do I always come off looking like a bad person? I'm not going to hurt him.'

Mum faltered, 'It's just that since you started this church business, you've gone quite strange... I just want what's best for you. There aren't many men like Zack and your father around… '

'I wish you understood my faith–'

'I don't understand why you struggle so much with it though. Isn't faith meant to give you peace? Now, Vanessa, she doesn't seem to struggle like you do.'

I carried on wiping down the kitchen sink. 'Mum, Zack and I are fine. Stop fretting. And leave Vanessa out of this. It's not a competition.'

'It's just that I worry about you. You're my only child.'

Child. I'm 28. Okay, so I make a mess of my life – but I don't expect my parents to clean up after me.

Zack smiled at me from the living room and I smiled back at him. I still can't believe he's mine. Why is he with me? I'm hardly the world's most tolerable person. There are times I'm so wracked with guilt, I'm convinced I'm the world's greatest fraud. But when Zack puts his arm around me, I know as surely as the sky is blue that I don't want to be anywhere else.

The truth is, there is nothing I fear more than being alone. I envy my parents. Their love story and the life they live… I want something like that. Very badly. Is that so bad? I have a recurring nightmare that I'm 40 years old, single, and trying hard to convince myself that I'm content that way because that's what people expect from me. Well, maybe some people are content like that – but not me. Why is that so hard for people to understand? Being with Zack shows me that there's so much more to life than I have been experiencing in my small world.

Yet, even as I sometimes wish I'd never set foot inside a church, at the same time I thank God with all my heart for this faith that threatens to cause me much unhappiness.

As I squeezed out the dishcloth and returned to the living room, smiling at Zack, I felt suddenly overwhelmed with depression. Why do I keep on lying to myself? I'm not comfortable with the choices I've made regarding Zack and God – yet I'm not willing to go back on it.

When we got back to Zack's, I clung to him for dear life.

'Kemi, you shouldn't take your Mum's lectures so seriously. You know she means well. Don't be upset.'

Dear Zack. Dear, dear Zack.

'I'm okay. Actually, I've got to go to Vanessa's. I forgot to mention it earlier. Church business... no big deal.'

'No worries. I'll drop you off... '

'No!'

He looked at me quizzically and then his face hardened.

'Fine,' he said. 'I'll see you later. That's, if you come back.'

I wanted to hold him and never let him go but I needed to talk to someone. Being Sunday, Vanessa's parents weren't in when I got there and I knew they wouldn't be back till late.

Vanessa didn't say anything when she saw me on her doorstep. She let me in and made me an extra strong coffee.

'There, I think you need this,' she said, handing me the mug.

I took it gratefully. 'Thanks.'

We sat awkwardly in silence for a few moments.

'How was the service? I didn't stay till the end.'

'It was fine. Pastor Michael says "hi".' Vanessa leaned forward. 'He's worried about you.'

'I'm worried about me.'

Now that I was at Vanessa's, I wanted to leave. I didn't know anyone else who could condemn people just by virtue of being herself. Do I mean 'condemn' or 'convict'?

'How's Zack?'

'Fine. Says hi.'

'Kemi–'

'Vanessa–'

We both laughed self-consciously.

'You first,' I said.

'What are you doing?' she asked, gently.

'I wish I knew.'

'You know, this is not God's best for you.'

I could see she was really trying hard to understand but if I didn't understand it myself, how could I explain it to someone else?

'Well, I'm sorry, Vanessa, but not everyone is blessed with praying parents and automatic rights to Christian marital bliss!'

'Why do you always throw that at me?'

'Because I need to remind you what *real* people go through in the *real* world. Zack might not be a Christian but he's not the devil incarnate either.'

She looked a bit stung at that. I suppose it was a bit harsh.

'You're still sleeping with him, aren't you?'

I didn't answer. Like it was her business! Maybe if she dipped her pure foot in the cesspit of humanity otherwise known as the real world, she would see things from my point of view. It's alright for her. Mark's the boy next door. He was handed to her on a plate all Christianised and ready to go. Not everyone's that fortunate. I pictured the Sanctifieds and heard them chorusing: 'God satisfies all my needs'. Gag!

'Kemi, trust God. Remember what the Bible says: all his promises are yes and amen–'

'Zack proposed to me and I said no.'

That shut her up.

'I love Zack. I really do, and it hurts that he doesn't trust me. He's always watching me, thinking I'll go running back to church because I feel so guilty about us. I know I've hurt him and I cannot even guarantee I won't hurt him again but things have gone so far that I cannot even contemplate giving him up. We're... we're living together now. Well, kind of. Okay, we're more or less living together. I don't really know how I got here. I guess I wanted to prove to him how far I was willing to go for us.'

I couldn't look into Vanessa's eyes because I knew what I would find there: a whole range of hostile emotions but especially disappointment. Whatever our differences, I knew all she had ever wanted was God's best for me.

'Kemi, I'm going to ask you again: what are you doing? If you don't want to marry him, why are you with him?'

'I don't know. I can't marry him because he's not a Christian and I don't want to give up our relationship because I... I... I can't. And please don't ask me to. Vanessa, you have to help me. I'm really confused.'

'You're not confused. You know perfectly well what you're doing. You made a choice, Kemi Smith. You made that choice when you went to his office a few weeks ago and spent the night with him and you've been consciously making the same choice every day. I know you think I live in a spiritual bubble but I'm not stupid.'

Why did I think she would understand?

Just then, the key turned in the front door. Her Triple S parents were back from church. Uncle Daniel came bounding in full of Holy Ghost goodness. When he saw me in the living room, he gave me the biggest smile this side of heaven.

'Well, if it isn't Ms Marketing Guru Director herself! We don't see much of you these days. Where've you been?'

Aunty Sandra came in behind him, also full of smiles. I allowed myself to be hugged, prodded and teased by the two of them. They loved me. These people had a heart for God, for me, for my family. I knew Vanessa hadn't told them about Zack and me. I decided there and then that they wouldn't find out. I needed them not to think badly of me.

Vanessa and I didn't talk much after her parents arrived. We'd said all that needed saying. I stayed for another half an hour before going home – to my flat. I needed to think. I called Zack to tell him where I was.

'Are you coming back?' he asked me.

He still didn't trust me. I could still walk away.

'Yes,' I replied. 'I'm coming back. I just need to pick up a few things.'

Monday July 2

Why are you downcast, O my soul? Why so disturbed within me? (Psalm 42:11).

Life goes on. The Marketing Director officially announced his resignation this morning. Forty-five and tired of the rat race.

I'm not going to think about Vanessa. Who does she think she is, passing judgement on me like that? Well, I'm sorry Ms 'I'm-so-perfect-I-never-make-any-mistakes', but life in the real world involves making choices that one wouldn't ordinarily indulge, let alone think about. I can't deal with my faith – it's been a struggle from day one. Living for Someone I can't see? All I ask for is an appearance now and then. I'm not asking for the moon.

I repeat: I am an only child. Wonderful though my parents are, I need more to sustain me in this journey I call life. Interestingly eccentric as my cousins are, I want someone of my very own. If I stay in church, I will not find that person. Period. And why should I have to choose between love and faith anyway?

I wish I didn't have to work. It's such a drag. Who cares about singing nappies when your whole life is falling apart? And, yes, the Star Baby competition is still going ahead. It's going to be an utter disaster. I can just imagine the backlash against Singing Diapers. Everyone's going to think they're heartless publicity-hungry people who'll do anything to sell their products. (Which they are, of course, but they could go about it another way.)

I need inspiration for a new campaign. One so good, Windy CEO will have no choice but to forsake Star Baby. *Think, Kemi, think!* Dear Lord... What am I doing? Like he's really going to listen to me? I'm a sinner! *Think, Kemi!* If I cannot even draw up a promotion campaign for a nappy company, what makes me think I can be a Marketing Director?

Zack's coming to pick me up after work and we'll go home together. Can't wait to see him and just have him hold me. What is wrong with that?

Later

That Zack! Just when I think he can't do any wrong, he goes and puts his foot in it. Would you believe, he turned up at my office with the woman from Camden? You know... the one who tried to fill my place when she thought I was gone; the Jezebel husband-stealer. As I stepped outside the office, there they were, waiting for me. When Zack saw me, he hurried to my side, put his arms around me and announced to the woman, 'Kemi – Maxine. Maxine – Kemi.' And stood there smiling like this was meant to be one normal get together... Which it definitely wasn't. I couldn't believe how clueless Zack was being. What did he think he would accomplish doing this?

I gave 'Maxine' a fixed grin and said, 'Hi.'

'Hi yourself! Zack's told me so much about you. I think I saw you in Camden, preaching or something like that?'

'I believe that Jesus Christ is Lord and Saviour,' I said loudly. Her smile evaporated.

I turned to Zack, 'Darling, we must go now. My parents are waiting.'

Holding his arm, I turned firmly towards the tube station.

He turned to Maxine and said, apologetically, 'Sorry. It seems I have to go. And I was so looking forward to you guys meeting each other. Another time, eh?'

'Try Armageddon,' I gritted through my teeth.

'Pardon?'

'Sorry, Zack, just remembered something. Now, we really must go. Nice meeting you, Maxine!' And I turned my man firmly and resolutely away from Maxine. I was still in a mood when we got home.

'I just don't see what the problem is, Kemi! I thought you guys would get on. She's a great colleague. She's really nice!'

'She fancies you! You can't be that blind. Come on!'

'You think every woman on the street fancies me.'

'Maybe if you were a bit more circumspect with your relationships, I wouldn't feel like this.'

'Maybe if you weren't so wracked with guilt about being with me, we wouldn't be having this conversation. You wouldn't marry me; you can't decide whether or not you want to have a relationship with me and apparently you don't even trust me!'

'Look, I don't want you to leave! I've given up God for you—'

'I'm not going anywhere, Kemi Smith. I'm going to ask you one last time: what do you want?'

'You, Zack! You!'

Zack threw his hands in the air. 'I don't know what to say or do anymore. I'm trying really hard to understand but it seems like everything I do is wrong. I give up. I'm sleeping on the sofa tonight. I think you need some time alone.'

I went into the bedroom and slammed the door after me. Who to talk to? Foluke. She'll cheer me up. I need a dose of craziness in my life.

Tuesday July 3

'Are you the king of the Jews?' 'Yes, it is as you say,' Jesus replied (Matthew 27:11).

Yes, King of Kings and Lords of Lords. That's who Jesus is. That's who I need. Dear God, I am so sorry that I've made a mess of everything. Thing is, I've gone too far to come back. I can't give Zack up. I can't. This is so hard.

Zack apologised about Maxine. Said he could see my point. I apologised for acting like a leech. One thing's for sure, Maxine's out of the picture. He won't be trying to have us meet as 'friends' in a hurry. So I suppose something good came out of last night.

Forgive me, Lord, but I refuse to share Zack. He's all I've got now.

When I got to work, I ran to the loo and opened up my Bible. I opened it at one of my all-time favourite verses: Psalm 37:4 – *Delight yourself in the LORD and he will give you the desires of your heart.* Somehow it didn't comfort me like it normally did. I delight in you, Lord. But I also delight in Zack. Where does that leave me? Lead me, Lord, to make the right decision. I feel such a heaviness around me. Help me, Lord. I feel like I'm falling. Hold me in your arms and surround me with the sweet presence of the Holy Spirit. I am so scared.

Almost two weeks since my victory meeting with Windy CEO and I haven't produced a progress report on how the campaign's going. The market research company's messing up. What could be so hard about calling a few hundred people and asking them if they would support such a thing as Star Baby? Even I could do that.

Sharronne and I are just ignoring each other now. I ignore her for the simple reason that I don't quite have the energy to deal with her. I saw her practising her wily skills on James, the person I replaced her with. Really, the girl needs lessons in subtlety. Thank God, James is wiser. He's *many* things but he's also a married man with a year-old son. You would think Sharronne would choose her prey more sensibly.

I had a meeting with Amanda about the Marketing Director post.

'I think you'll do well,' she said to me.

I just don't understand Amanda. She veers between an Amazonian and Mother Theresa, and it's quite hard to keep up

74

with the changes. I still cannot comprehend the attraction between her and Robert but I'm quite chuffed inside that I had a small part to play in getting them together. It's always nice to bring people some form of relational happiness.

Vanessa sent me a text message. I JST WNT U 2 NO I'M ALWAYS HERE 4 U. I didn't bother replying. It seems everyone but me knows what's good for me. I know what's good for me: Zack, my beloved prince and my brick. Even if all I ever bring him is pure strife. I'm sure he rues the day he ever laid eyes on me.

'Not at all,' he said when I called him at work to confirm (as if didn't have anything else to do at work). 'I've never regretted meeting you.'

Yeah, right.

Back to Singing Diapers. Lord, give me a campaign that will blow their socks off. Holy Spirit, inspire me. Let your creativity flow through my mind.

End of working day

Nothing. Nothing. No inspiration. The Singing Diapers Star Baby competition is here to stay. Thing is, I have no idea how to develop the detail of the competition and apparently I'm the brains behind it. Oh Lord, what have I got myself into?

Wednesday July 4

When a prophet of the LORD *is among you, I reveal myself to him in visions, I speak to him in dreams (Numbers 12:6).*

Vanessa texted me again last night. She wants to know if I'll be coming to the prayer meeting on Friday. I didn't reply and made up my mind there and then not to go. I didn't want everyone looking at me and judging me for staying with Zack.

They judge me, Lord. I see it in their eyes when I slip into the service on Sundays just as the sermon's about to start. I feel their eyes on my back when I slip out just before the end of the sermon.

Lord, I'm so weak. Steady me. I've gone too far, Lord. I cannot go back.

Got to work early again this morning, ran to the loo and devoured my Bible. Jesus did not condemn the adulterous woman (John 8:10,11). So... that means that he won't condemn me either. But, there again, he also told the woman to 'leave her life of sin'. Well, I'm not leaving Zack and that's that.

Spent the whole day head down at my desk. The market research company emailed me their findings. It seems I was wrong. People are willing to do anything to be famous these days – even sacrificing their children's purity on the altar of Star Baby. The public were asked what a Star Baby competition should consist of and they all said music. When reminded that the babies in question had an age ceiling of one year, they weren't so forthcoming with suggestions. Makes two of us.

Amanda and Robert invited me and Zack to dinner at their place on Friday. I wasn't even sure they were living together. I said yes and hoped frantically that Zack didn't have anything planned. I wondered why they asked us. To be frank, I don't think of our relationship extending beyond the office building.

Those two defy definition.

Star Baby. Lord, I need a competition that will stand apart from other baby competitions. I need a competition that will, quite simply, make the other brands wish they'd never even thought about going into the baby products market. I guess what I'm trying to say is: Lord, I need your help.

I can't get that adulterous woman out of my head. Did she go back to the married man?

'Does it matter?' I can hear Vanessa ask. That girl. I'm not going to call her. I'm not. Had a quick natter with Foluke at lunchtime. She said she was happy that I was happy and that she didn't understand the fuss about Zack and me. When I told her Zack proposed to me and I turned him down, she said she didn't understand why I was still with him if I didn't believe we had a future together.

'Anyway,' she continued, 'who am I to talk? I'm usually one step from away from total disaster. It's a shame, though. I was really starting to think the church stuff was for real. I was even wondering if maybe I should go in that direction. But if you, of all people, don't really know what you're doing, then I guess people like me don't have any hope at all. Never mind, it was nice while it lasted. Anyway, bye!'

I couldn't answer. I couldn't believe that someone thought about me the way I thought about Vanessa, that Foluke had briefly thought of me like the Triple S People with their direct links to heaven while the rest of us scramble on earth looking for the wires to hook us up to the source.

I couldn't leave the office. There was too much to do. I couldn't call Vanessa after all that's happened recently between us. And I certainly couldn't call Zack. I dialled Pastor Michael's number and hung up when he picked up the phone. No, not Pastor Michael. I didn't want him looking into my spirit and seeing my sins in all their fleshly glory. He was a kind and wonderful man, but my recent lifestyle choice automatically ruled out sympathetic conversation with him. Definitely not Pastor Michael. The Sanctifieds? No, not them either. I ruled them out of my world the minute I went back to Zack. My parents? No, definitely not. I'm trying to live like a responsible 28-year-old and not go running to them every time I scrape my knee.

And I'm not talking to you either, God, because I know you're not pleased with me.

I can't believe this is what it comes down to: I have no one to talk to. Not even God. Seems like everywhere I turn I see people I've hurt: Zack, Vanessa, Pastor Michael, Vanessa's parents, Foluke. Even my parents. I'm sure they think I'm a disappointment. All they ever wanted was for me to settle down. But no, I had to become a Pentecostal Christian and turn everyone crazy. God help me.

The Singing Diapers account is driving me nuts. Lord, I know I'm not your favourite person at the moment but if you could just give me a bit of inspiration on this one, it would be most appreciated.

Thursday July 5

I am the first and I am the last; apart from me there is no God (Isaiah 44:6).

The phone rang while we were at home this evening. Zack spoke to whoever was on the other end for a few minutes before passing the phone to me. 'Vanessa,' he mouthed. I was irritated. What did she want?

'Vanessa, I'm not coming to the prayer meeting tomorrow

night so don't even bother trying to change my mind,' I said. I felt Zack tense up so I took the phone to the bedroom.

'Just hear me out, Kemi. I'm not sorry for what I said on Sunday because it's the truth but I am sorry for the way I said it. It didn't come out the way it was meant to. And I'm sorry for treating Zack like the devil. He's one of the kindest men I know and I have nothing against him. You know that. So, please forgive me. If not for the sake of our friendship then for the sake of my parents. I know you can't stand me at the moment, but you love my parents and... well, it would be good if you could forgive me.'

I pursed my lips. Like it was that easy? She of all people should know the power of words. Wasn't she a preacher's daughter?

'I apologised to Zack when he picked up the phone,' Vanessa continued when I didn't answer.

'I'm still not coming to the prayer meeting.' I meant it. Besides, I was going to Amanda and Robert's for dinner. What would that be like? They would probably feed us sushi and raw vegetables or something. I'll just make sure Zack and I eat something before we go.

'Fine,' said Vanessa. 'But can we still meet up? I've missed hanging out with you... and, by the way, the wedding's back on.'

'Really? Why didn't you say?! Vanessa, that's great news!'

'Yeah,' She sounded coy. 'We're thinking December. Will you be maid of honour? I'm also thinking of going back to work. I've had enough time out. I'm bored and putting on weight. Anyway, what are you doing after the service on Sunday? We could meet up.'

'Wow! Maid of honour! No, not Sunday. But soon. I'll call you over the weekend.'

'No probs. Speak to you later. Bye!'

Vanessa. I really don't know how or why God put us together as friends because I don't understand our relationship. Seems like I shall have to drop going to church completely. I don't think I could bear being with Vanessa and having all those people coming to congratulate her after the service on her choice of a godly husband – and wondering why I missed out so spectacularly!

When I went back to the sitting room, Zack pulled me close to him. 'You guys made it up yet?' he asked.

'Yes,' I replied, marvelling at how handsome and wonderful he was.

'Good. Because I don't like it when you guys argue. You turn into a witch.' And he kissed me.

Friday July 6

Make every effort to live in peace with all men and to be holy; without holiness no one will see the Lord (Hebrews 12:14).

I got into work today at 7am. Today is Amanda and Robert's dinner day. Also Singing Diapers Star Baby competition countdown day. Yes, indeedy! This is the day I'm supposed to pull the strands of the Star Baby competition project plan together like the hard-working advertising person I am. This is the day I'm supposed to prove my worth to Amanda and let her know that her faith in me is well invested. This is the day I hope I don't get fired. Am I stressed? Nope. Because I can do all things through Christ who strengthens me and enables me to soar like an eagle. Even when it's blatantly obvious to everyone but myself that I'm not doing any flying or soaring at the moment.

Where is the blinding flash of inspiration when you need it?

Then, over my first cup of coffee of the day, I got it. Babies would audition to 'sing' as a group for a music CD for babies (that would tie in with the musical note concept of Singing Diapers). They would be backed with a philharmonic orchestra or something. The best babies from the regional rounds would make the final group. Sort of like *Pop Idol* but better.

Of course this means that the competition had better be called Star Babies rather than Star Baby. The babies qualifying for the final rounds would get a year's free supply of Singing Diapers products, and the winners would become the faces of Singing Diapers and whatever else James and my team could concoct. You know – the full range of merchandise opportunities: posters, calendars, toddler t-shirts, rattle toys, musical toys, Star Baby dolls for little girls to dress in mini Singing Diapers.

I could just see it: five gap-toothed babies cooing their baby coos to Mozart softly played behind, maybe with a full orchestra, perhaps some tracks with just those medieval wind instruments. It would be a blast. THANK YOU, JESUS!! What an inspiration! I quickly summoned James and told him the ideas – which he loved. He asked if his child could enter the competition under another name as apparently the little thing has a gorgeous giggle. I refused. Doesn't he understand 'conflicting interests'?

We got down to business. We put together a project plan with the launch date for Star Babies scheduled for next month. We'd be pushing it, but Windy CEO was really insistent on capturing the Christmas market. It also means kissing a normal life and sleep goodbye for the next couple of months but I think I can do it. I'll take myself to a retreat when it's all over. I was excited at the meeting. I was back on top. This is what marketing is all about. Giving people choices.

Thank you, Lord. Today is indeed a good day. And now for dinner at Amanda's...

Later

Wonders will never cease. Amanda and Robert asked Zack and me to be their witnesses at their registry office wedding in a month's time.

'That's not why I put you forward for the Marketing Director post,' Amanda added archly when I sat there stumped at her request.

'I know. I just don't understand why you chose me. I didn't even think you liked me,' I stuttered.

'I don't have many friends,' she replied and left it at that.

But what about family, siblings and all the rest of that? You must have someone! I wanted to cry out but Zack gave me a very loud 'shut your mouth' look. I complied.

'Aren't you even going to ask me about Zack?' I asked Amanda when she showed me the bathroom.

'No. Not really because I'm not interested,' she replied. I came to the conclusion that she and Robert were two of a kind. That maybe they deserved each other. Being off their rockers and all. And, yes, we had sushi and raw vegetables accompanied with sparkling organic herb cordial.

Saturday July 7

The LORD will cause men to hear his majestic voice and will make them see his arm coming down with raging anger and consuming fire, with cloudburst, thunderstorm and hail (Isaiah 30:30).

I've decided not to go to church anymore. I can have a relationship with God outside of church. I'm sick and tired of sneaking in and out like a criminal. People don't approve of my relationship with Zack and I'm not going anywhere he's not accepted, so there.

When I told Vanessa about this decision she said, 'No one is condemning you. You're the one condemning yourself and I wish you would stop pointing the judgement finger at everyone else because *you're* doing what you accuse other people of doing. It's tedious, it's boring and I wish you would just get a grip.'

I hung up. (Was hanging up on Vanessa becoming the norm or what?) I wasn't in the mood.

A minute later, my mobile rang again. It was one of the Sanctifieds. Her mother had left the women's refuge and gone back to her dad, she said. She was worried about her. She hoped I didn't mind but she needed legal advice and she knew Zack was a barrister. She was planning to go and check on her mum and two younger sisters – one's 12 and the other's 13. She has two guys from church with her just in case her father turns violent. Which apparently is not unusual. She was wanting to know, does she have any rights under the law to take her siblings away from her parents if she thinks they're in danger? I passed the phone to Zack. He was very subdued when he came off the phone.

'Some people spend thousands and thousands of pounds on IVF and other treatments just to have children. They put their lives at risk sometimes because they want to have babies so badly and even then, the treatments often fail. Other people are fortunate enough to conceive easily, only to make the children wish they'd never been born. Some other people don't even give their child a chance to live because the child doesn't fit into their current life plan. Then there are others who give birth and vanish, abandoning their children. The children grow up wondering, "Who am I?" and "Why am I here?" I don't know. What's it all about?'

'There are people who bring children into the world and love them and nurture them the way God intended.'

'Like your parents.'

'Like my parents,' I repeated firmly. I held onto his arm.

'Kemi, if we have kids, I wouldn't be able to tell them about my side of the family because I don't know anything about them. Nothing. Absolutely nothing! I don't even know what my mother or father looks like. I don't know if my mother is manic-depressive or if my father's a rapist. My mother left me outside an orphanage and vanished. Just like that.'

'Zack, I know who you are. God knows who you are.'

'This same God you can't bear to face because you're with me?'

Everything comes back to him – God.

'No, Zack, this same God who loves you like I love you.'

'This same God who was there when my baby was killed?'

I knew what he was referring to but I couldn't help him. My heart bled for him though.

'Zack...'

'Don't worry. I'm okay.' He paused for a minute.

'Your friend's sisters have to stay with their parents. I told her to let the Social Services know if she thought they were in danger. She refused. They would take her sisters away and separate them, she said. I told her that wasn't necessarily true. She said she wasn't quite sure what her father would do if he found out she'd been blabbing to outsiders, which is why she wanted to know if she could take care of them herself. Your friend is 25 and she lives in a one-bedroom council flat on a notorious estate in east London. She's a checkout girl at her local supermarket and studying part-time. Her idea is not only not feasible but totally impractical.'

He stood up. 'You've got the most amazing parents in the world. Don't forget that.'

I went for a walk after that. I needed to clear my head. Why are some people blessed with so much and some have so little? I couldn't help thinking about Zack in that orphanage as a child, hoping that someday someone would come and take him 'home' to be in a proper family. But those people never came. I marvel at how well he turned out. I came to the conclusion that I was the most selfish person in the whole world. So much going for me. So many advantages. Surrounded by people with needs that I can't possibly help with, let alone handle myself. And I'm throwing tantrums because I think people want my boyfriend? Selfish, selfish, selfish!

The walk did me good. I called my parents as soon as I got back. I wanted them to know I loved them and appreciated everything they'd done for me.

'Kemi Smith, I don't know what's come over you but I suggest you get a hold of yourself right this very minute,' my mother ordered when I started blubbing. 'And put Zack on the phone.'

Zack listened for a few minutes then said, 'She's been a bit stressed out lately. And I think it's that time of the month as well. Uh... uh... okay. I'll talk to you later.' He turned to me. 'She said you should get a grip.'

I wish I *could* get a grip. No, I'm not having my period. I'm just hormonal. That and the fact that I think I *do* want to marry Zack.

I'm going to church tomorrow. I have to. There's so much going on inside my head and, let's face it, I need help. The only place I've been able to get sensible help has been the church. (Translation: Pastor Michael.)

Sunday July 8

... the LORD longs to be gracious to you; he rises to show you compassion (Isaiah 30:18).

My day went something like this: I bounded out of bed and got ready for church. I opened the front door and was confronted with the kind of ferocious rain known only to London residents in the summertime. I bounded upstairs to get my umbrella and was about to bound down the stairs and out of the door when Zack opened the bedroom door still in his pyjamas and called after me.

'I'll take you. It's raining and I don't want you turning up at the church looking like a drowned rat. Your friends might accuse your heathen boyfriend of not taking care of you. Then it'll turn to accusations of murder if you catch your death of cold.' But he was smiling when he said it.

'I have another idea. Why don't you come to church with me?'

'Just hang on a minute.'

He dropped me off at church. I saw Vanessa and Mark on my way in. Mark waved to me and I smiled at him. Vanessa ignored me. That hurt. I wished things were the way they used to be before all this stuff about Zack happened. Life was a lot less complicated then. I didn't wait for the sermon to finish before running down to the pastor's office. I wanted to be the first in line. I should have known a million other people would have the same idea as me. Actually, there were six other people waiting outside his office when I got there. I couldn't believe it. If their sessions with Pastor Michael were anything like mine, I calculated I would probably have to wait about three hours for a chance to talk to him. Not that I even knew what I wanted to talk about. I guess I just wanted to talk to someone, anyone, about anything and he was the only person I could think of who would listen without condemnation.

I love Zack but I also need people to talk to. Thing is, I'm so paranoid that I can't bear to open up to anyone. Then I thought, have I once today spared a thought for the Sanctified battling to save her family from a deranged maniac? Nope. Everything I do revolves around me. Me. Me. Me.

Lord, I'm such a failure. I've messed up. I chose Zack over you. He's not a Christian. I cannot marry someone who doesn't share my faith. A house that is divided cannot stand.

Beloved, why are you with him then?

Because I love him.

I made my way out of the church, weighed down by terrible guilt. I couldn't help thinking of the Love Chapter in the Bible, 1 Corinthians 13: *Love is patient, love is kind. It does not envy, it does not boast, it is not proud. It is not rude, it is not self-seeking, it is not easily angered, it keeps no record of wrongs. Love does not delight in evil but rejoices with the truth.* Did I really love Zack or was I seeking to fulfil my own selfish desires?

When I got home, Zack had Sunday lunch roasting away quite

nicely in the oven. The gastronomic smell permeated the flat. My tummy growled but I felt sick. I didn't want to eat.

'I called your parents and told them we wanted to have our very own special Sunday lunch. What do you think?' He gestured towards the oven and smirked. 'Bet you didn't think I could do this.'

When I didn't answer, he looked at my face more closely and asked, 'Do you want to talk about it?'

'Zack, why are you with me?'

'Because I love you, you dope, and I don't want anyone else.'

'Even if I don't want to marry you?'

'Even that. Yes.'

'Zack, where are we going?'

'I don't know but we're not going to waste any time talking about this today. I've made lunch. We're going to eat, watch *EastEnders* and I'll fall asleep on the sofa and you'll have a fit, like you do every weekend, because I'll drool all over it.'

I smiled sadly. What have I done to this man?

'Come here.' He held out his hand. I took it and he pulled me into his arms. My rock, my brick, my prince. My very own Zack.

Monday July 9

A wicked messenger falls into trouble, but a trustworthy envoy brings healing (Proverbs 13:17).

Sharronne came to my desk as soon as she saw me come into the office. I was mildly irritated. I had a lot to accomplish today and the last thing I needed was an insubordinate junior trying to grovel but making it seem like she wasn't. Especially now that everyone knows I am up for the Marketing Director post. I've said it once and I'll say it again: the girl needs lessons in subtlety.

'Hi Kemi! Just wanted to say congratulations on the Marketing Director post–'

'I haven't got it yet. I'm just up for it. There's a difference,' I snapped.

Her smile faltered but, like a cat, she picked herself up again. 'Yes, I know. I just wanted to be the first to congratulate you. I'm sure you'll get it.'

'We'll see. Anything else?'

'Uh, no. Okay. Guess I'll see you later.'

After she left, I delved into my Bible. Re today's verse, she definitely isn't trustworthy and most definitely was not on a healing mission when she came to see me.

Foluke sent me an e-card. *To the best cousin in the world,* it says. *You rock!!* I sent her an email and told her to go get herself a job. 'Now that she's more normal, I don't have to keep on supporting her financially, do I?' her father asked me when he called last week. I told him not to worry, that I would talk to her. I'm sure she'll see sense. She's 35 years old. Time for her to soar like an eagle out of her parents' nest. It's either that or life on the pavement.

Next visitor – James. 'Kemi, my wife really wants James Junior to take part in Star Babies. She said, maybe you were limiting your options. What people won't know won't hurt, will it?'

I didn't bother replying. I beamed up a short prayer for patience and concentrated on the Star Babies project plan, the detail of which, incidentally, was James' responsibility, but I figured he was too raw from rejection to work on it.

Then I got an internal email from Amanda. *Could you pop into my office for a few minutes?* I looked at my desk and the floor area around my chair. There was paper everywhere: market research reports, sales forecasts for Singing Diapers, campaign costs, competitor's market reports and several petitions from philharmonic orchestras clamouring to work on the Star Babies project. I gritted my teeth. I didn't particularly want to see Amanda but wouldn't it be easier if she called by my desk instead of emailing me? Whatever happened to the personal touch?

Before I could phrase a good reply there was another email. From Amanda. *In the next 10 seconds, preferably.* Oh Lord, why did I agree to be her wedding witness? I hurried to her office, knocked and stepped inside expecting a tongue-lashing on my speed of response to her emails. Except Amanda was behind the door in a wedding dress trying very, very hard not to look sheepish!

'I couldn't resist. I had to,' she said.

So she was human after all! I was still smiling when I went back to my desk ten minutes later. I dialled Vanessa's mobile to share the moment with her, then remembered how she ignored me in church yesterday so I hung up. I tried Zack's work number but it went to voicemail. I thought about calling Mum but decided against it. The moment had passed. Still, it brought a smile to my face every time I thought about it during the day.

Tuesday July 10

The eyes of the LORD are everywhere, keeping watch on the wicked and the good (Proverbs 15:3).

Work was crazy the rest of the day. Got home at 10pm last night! Zack was sprawled on the sofa, totally oblivious to the world. I turned off the TV and made my way to the kitchen intending to feast on Sunday's lunch remnants when my mobile rang. Mark's number flashed on the screen. I was tired so I didn't pick it up. It went to voicemail. I checked it later.

'Hello Kemi, it's Mark. Hope you're okay. I wish you and Vanessa would make up. You know she means well and, for her, that means living God's way.'

I deleted it.

Friday July 13

Arise, shine, for your light has come, and the glory of the LORD rises upon you (Isaiah 60:1).

Today is Friday 13th and, according to today's Bible verse, it's also the day that the Lord's glory will shine on me. Er, don't think so. Don't know if I should go to tonight's prayer meeting or not. I just know everyone's going to be staring at me: the black sheep of the congregation.

Kemi, get a grip! Not everyone's life revolves around you and (though you'll probably find this weird) people have more earth-shaking things to do and think about than you, Zack and your sex life.

Right. I get it. I'm not important.

Oh, just shut up and get to work!!

I really hate it when I start talking to myself. *Focus, Kemi, focus!* You have a campaign worth several million pounds to deal with. YOU HAVEN'T GOT TIME TO THINK ABOUT YOUR NON-POSITION IN THE WORLD. MOVE IT, GIRL!!

Later

I moved it. I worked like a maniac until it was 6pm, then I called Vanessa. Couldn't help it. I missed her. Terribly.

'Why did you ignore me in church?!' I squelched down the phone as soon as she picked up.

'Because you're behaving like a kid and driving me nuts. I told you the wedding was back on and all you did was talk about how the church hated you. You might find this really weird but I do need your support sometimes as well.'

'Really?' I didn't believe her. After all, she was Vanessa, Jesus' blood sister.

'Of course! And I know Mark called you even though I specifically asked him not to. Anyway, I can't talk right now. I'm applying for some jobs.'

Lord, I hope you give Vanessa the job she deserves. She's a good girl. Rather unlike me and, despite her many weaknesses (read: ability to irritate the living daylights out of me), she's actually okay. I'm sorry for not being considerate about her wedding. I just couldn't face the idea that she would be comparing her God-sent, angel-on-a-mission, vision-inspired wedding to the life I've chosen to live with Zack. Not that she would do that anyway because she's Jesus' blood sister.

I'm so selfish. Vanessa's right. All I ever think about is myself. I wish I wasn't like this. Maybe, if I went on a lone mission evangelising in Camden, then God would love me. Or maybe I should spend some time with my parents this weekend. Maybe I should stop thinking and go home. It's Friday 13th after all.

2am

Can't sleep. Decided to spend a couple of nights back in my

own flat, the bed's too big and I miss Zack. I've called him 50 million times already. He didn't answer his phone the 49,999,999th time I rang. And they say true love waits. Anyway, I want to know if I can survive not being with Zack (not that he knows that). Who am I trying to kid? I know I can't. I'm one step away from calling a cab to take me back to his flat.

Have to talk to Foluke about her being financially responsible.

3am

Still can't sleep so read the Love Chapter of the Bible again. But don't think I'll read it anymore. It makes me feel guilty. I think I'll go evangelising by myself tomorrow. Not Camden. Somewhere else. Kentish Town maybe? Or even Holloway Road. Nothing like preaching the gospel alongside dodgy people selling dodgy tobacco masquerading as cigarettes. On second thoughts, that might not be a good idea. Don't really fancy being torn to shreds by dodgy people selling dodgy cigarettes on dodgy streets. All in all, a very dodgy idea.

Saturday July 14

Love and faithfulness meet together; righteousness and peace kiss each other (Psalm 85:10).

Didn't go to Kentish Town to evangelise, nor to Holloway Road, nor anywhere else for that matter. BECAUSE I WOKE UP AT MIDDAY!! Couldn't believe I slept that late. Then my parents came round. Foluke came as well and so did Vanessa. And get this: Pastor Michael called me. Said he just wanted to check I was okay and he hoped I didn't mind but he would like to meet the person that's causing me so much emotional and spiritual turmoil. That's Zack. Couldn't believe it. I told him I would discuss it with Zack but that the answer would probably be no. He said no problem and he hoped to see me in church on Sunday.

Pastor Michael is a really nice fella. And I have missed talking to him. He's really kind. I'll tell Zack and, hopefully, he'll say yes and come with me. I can't wait for us to do that.

Anyway, Dad sorted my leaking kitchen sink, while in the sitting room Mum regaled Foluke, Vanessa and me with how she found Dad half-dead in Liverpool 30 years ago. She sure is fond of that story but that's okay.

'I wasn't half-dead,' Dad called out indignantly from the kitchen. 'I was heartsick!'

'Yes, half-dead and heartsick!!' Mum retorted, before we all fell onto the carpet laughing.

'But how did you know Uncle was *The One?* I can't believe you left friends and family for him,' Foluke said.

'I wasn't thinking about him being *The One*. I just wanted to be with him. I was 16. It was the 70s. Or maybe it was the Afro that did it.'

'Just my hair?' Dad called from under the sink.

Mum pretended she hadn't heard him. 'I guess I felt sorry for him. All that trouble for me. The least I could do was marry him. Besides, no one else would have him.'

We all started laughing again, especially Dad until he bumped his head on the pipe he was trying to fix.

'I think I understand a little about your thing with Zack,' said Vanessa, when everyone else had left. 'It's your parents. Just being around them, no one could help but yearn for the same thing they have. I'm sorry for not being so understanding.'

She still didn't get it.

'Vanessa, it's not just that. I want to have someone of my own. Like you have Mark. Can you at least try to see things my way?'

'Kemi, can you at least try to see things God's way?'

'Vanessa, it's not just the sex. I love Zack.'

'It's about the sex and more. You told me yourself that sex creates a bond between two people and–'

'I know what I said.'

'You're not being fair to him. You're like two ships going in different directions. He doesn't share your faith and you don't want to marry him – so why are you together?'

'Because he's mine. And I want what my parents have and... I want Zack!'

'In 1 Corinthians 13–'

'Don't you dare start quoting the Bible to me.'

She was quiet for a few minutes.

'Kemi, God doesn't hate you. You trusted him for eternal life. Why do you think he wouldn't do this one thing for you?'

'You've always had Mark. You cannot possibly imagine what it's like to be 40 years old, in church and single, pretending to all and sundry that you're happy with being single. I see it in church every Sunday. Loneliness is a terrible thing. May you never experience it. And I'm sick and tired of people treating me like I have shingles because I'm single. Those days are over.'

'You're not 40.'

'But I will be 40 and single and lonely if I don't do this. Let's not argue about this anymore. We've only just made up.'

After today, I'm determined we won't have this conversation again. I've decided on the path I want to follow. What she does with my decision is up to her.

When she left, I read today's Bible verse again. Where is my light, Lord? Where is it?

Sunday July 15

Restore me and I will return, because you are the LORD my God. After I strayed, I repented; after I came to understand, I beat my breast (Jeremiah 31:18,19).

I am not going to church today. It's not like I can't worship God in the privacy of my own home. I've decided I'm not going to tell Zack about Pastor Michael's offer. What would they talk about? No way. I don't want anybody making Zack feel bad about us. I've done enough damage to the man already. We're just finding our rhythm. If Pastor Michael gets in there, it would just ruin everything between Zack and me. Plus, I don't want to give up sleeping with Zack. I might as well be honest: I like it and I don't want anyone dictating to me how I lead my life. And I don't feel guilty.

Thing is, why is it that whenever I think about this, God seems to be whispering in my ear or tapping on my shoulder? I just want to be left alone.

Okay. I'm crazy. Either way, I'm still not going to church. Neither am I having Sunday lunch with my parents or Zack. I'm going to stay in my flat all day today and go home to Zack tomorrow. Can't believe how much I've missed him.

Monday July 16

I will betroth you to me for ever; I will betroth you in righteousness and justice, in love and compassion (Hosea 2:19).

Maybe I ought to stop reading these Bible verses.

I emailed the Star Babies project plan to Windy CEO today. 'Good stuff, Kemi! Good stuff!' So now it's confirmed. I'm a star. Can't wait to see Zack. I've really missed him. But I'm glad I spent the weekend by myself. I just wanted to prove to myself that I could be without him, even if it's only for a couple of days.

'You *are* coming back, aren't you?' he asked when I asked him if he minded me spending the weekend in my flat.

I nodded.

'Then, there's no problem, is there? Besides, I can't wait to live like a bachelor again for a couple of days. You know, not shower, sleep and drool on the sofa and yes, the Sports Channel! Bring it on baby!'

Clearly, his needs are very simple.

Tuesday July 17

Come, let us go up to the mountain of the LORD, to the house of the God of Jacob. He will teach us his ways, so that we may walk in his paths (Isaiah 2:3).

I don't know what's come over Amanda. She giggles like a schoolgirl every time she sees me. Yesterday, she actually winked at me when she passed me in the corridor.

And, yes, Zack *did* miss me. When I went back home to his flat, everything was so clean and tidy I actually wondered if he had done everything he said he was going to.

'I did, but I didn't want World War Three to break out when you got back. You know how much of a cleanliness freak you are.'

If he knows that, why doesn't he clean and tidy up after himself all the time? But I kept my trap shut. We aren't married and I don't have the right to start behaving like his wife.

The Star Babies auditions start next week. Thankfully I don't actually have to be there, just running around back at the office pulling all the strings. It'll be chaos. The audition for the ten best will be shown live on TV, starting the first week of September. The final five babies that make it to the last round will be decided in the last week of November, with the winners' single scheduled for a Christmas release. I just know it'll be number one. Who can resist the cooing of toddlers against the background of the Leeds Philharmonic Orchestra? We had to choose the LPO in the end because Singing Diapers UK HQ is in Leeds. Windy CEO wouldn't have it any other way.

The phones are going crazy already. People from mums and toddlers' groups, fathers' rights groups, liberals, conservatives and all the national papers have been calling in for info. Their reaction to Star Babies has been mixed. I really thought Singing Diapers was going to be denounced as a baby-peddling organisation but no one has said any such thing. Yet. I think the general consensus is that Star Babies was inevitable. *A natural progression in the spate of recent reality industry entry shows,* wrote the *Guardian. What next? Star Foetus?* screamed the *Daily Mail.*

So, all in all, life is good.

I haven't told Zack about the pastor's invite. I don't know if I should.

Love is not self-seeking.

That Love Chapter again! I can't seem to get away from it. Alright, I think I *will* tell Zack about the invite. Maybe he'll be so bowled over by Pastor Michael's wisdom that he'll convert to Christianity. Wouldn't that be great?

Maybe so, but it would also mean giving up being intimate with each other. Do I really want to do that? Of course I do! Eternal life versus sleeping with Zack: it's a hard one.

What am I thinking?! *Focus, Kemi, focus!* Don't jump one millennium. Maybe I should just tell Zack about the pastor's invitation and stop worrying about 'what ifs'.

Amanda informed me this morning that the interview for the Marketing Director's post is in two weeks.

'You'll be okay,' she said and winked. I wish she would stop winking. When she first started, it was cute. Now it's just plain freaky.

I called Sharronne over to my desk.

'Do you know why I haven't taken disciplinary action against you for insubordination?' I asked her.

Her feline eyes narrowed and she tried to smile imploringly. It came out like a grimace.

'I'll tell you why,' I continued, not waiting for an answer. 'I think you have a lot of talent. I think you'll do well, but, if you're not careful, you'll find yourself out of this industry a lot sooner than you expect. You need to use your professional talents for your career instead of relying on your "other" talents to get you where you want to go. I say we start on a clean slate. What say you?'

She nodded, like I thought she would. It was easier than admitting her shortcomings to me.

'Great. Have a good day.'

She stumped back to her desk.

I think I handled that well, Lord. What do you think?

Wednesday July 18

Remember me... O my God, and show mercy to me according to your great love (Nehemiah 13:22).

I'm meeting Vanessa after work to discuss wedding stuff. I asked her to meet me at Zack's but she refused.

I didn't tell Zack about the pastor's invitation yesterday. I don't know why. I really wanted to but something held me back.

Sunday July 22

Blessed are you, O Israel! Who is like you, a people saved by the LORD? He is your shield and helper and your glorious sword (Deuteronomy 33:29).

Didn't go to church today. Zack offered to drive me but I refused. I'm not going back there again. I've decided it's not for me. I'll serve and worship God in the privacy of my own home. I don't need a building to do that. But I don't think I'll tell Vanessa just yet. Things are beginning to get back to normal between us. I'm so excited about being maid of honour, though Vanessa is rather more keen on lilac than I would like her to be.

Monday July 23

Even in laughter the heart may ache, and joy may end in grief (Proverbs 14:13).

The auditions for Star Babies started today.

James was beside himself when he got in to the office this afternoon, having checked out the London heats: 'The queues! Imagine it! Hundreds of ruby-cheeked and squalling kids all around the country with parents determined they'll be stars! It's great! Singing Diapers is on the map!!'

I felt my return grin turn into a sort of grimace when I remembered my interview for the Marketing Director post is in a week's time. I'm starting to feel nervous. But the feelgood factor from Star Babies ought to count for something. Amanda's wedding is the day after the interview. She's stopped winking at me, thank God. But Robert's been sort of swaggering around the office. Everyone's wondering what's wrong with the two of them. Everyone except me. I wished they hadn't asked Zack and me to be their witnesses. The whole office will know this time next week and tongues will wag. And I'm sure Sharronne will spearhead the 'That's-why-Amanda-put-Kemi-forward-for-the-Marketing-Director-post Campaign.'

But I don't care. I've survived worse storms than this. I'm an eagle soaring high in the sky. And, despite everything that's happened, I'm still a born-again, demon-kicking, tongue-lashing Pentecostal Nigerian. No one can hurt me.

Friday July 27

I have strayed like a lost sheep. Seek your servant, for I have not forgotten your commands (Psalm 119:176).

I think I'm pregnant...

Sunday July 29

The LORD will watch over your coming and going both now and for evermore (Psalm 121:8).

Sunday. A few months ago, Sundays filled me with such joy. It was all I could do to wait for the church service. But not anymore. Funny how so much can happen in five months.

I've been positively wretched to Zack all weekend. He thinks it's because I have my period. I *wish* I had my period. I've spent the whole weekend looking through my diary. There it was in black and white: the last time I had my period was May. Why didn't I notice?

I cannot be pregnant. I *can't* be. I left the flat this morning to go for a walk and found myself at the pharmacy. I was so embarrassed. I waited until the shop had cleared before shuffling in and asking for a pregnancy test pack. I had covered my hair and eyes with one of Zack's baseball caps. The pharmacist was unmoved. He'd obviously seen it all before.

'We can do the test here if you want. If you follow my wife, she'll tell you what to do. Don't worry – she's a pharmacist as well, so you'll be okay. That way, you won't have to take the test pack home. Just in case you don't want anyone to know,' he shrugged.

Just in case. I hadn't thought about that. Zack is very observant. If I took the test home, where would I hide it?

'It won't take a minute.' The woman pharmacist smiled reassuringly from behind the counter. A customer came inside the shop. I nodded. She opened a door behind the counter and I followed her.

The test was pointless. It confirmed what I already knew.

Monday July 30

Hear my prayer, O LORD, listen to my cry for help; be not deaf to my weeping. For I dwell with you as an alien... (Psalm 39:12).

My interview with the Board of Directors for the Marketing Director's post is at 11 this morning. I didn't sleep a wink last night.

Yesterday, when I got back from the pharmacy, I went straight to bed. Zack brought me a cup of tea.

'I'll tell your parents you're not feeling well today, that we can't make Sunday lunch.'

He put his palm against my forehead and frowned. 'You're not coming down with anything are you?'

I shook my head. I didn't trust myself to speak.

'Let me know if you need anything, okay?' He tucked me in bed and left the room. A few hours later, I heard him coming in to check up on me. I pretended I was asleep.

'I'll call Amanda and tell her they have to reschedule the interview,' he said later, as he was getting ready for bed.

'No, don't do that,' I said, smiling wanly. 'I'll be okay. It's probably all the stress of work.'

I didn't sleep. I looked at him as he slept beside me. *Oh God, what have I done? I will not think about this pregnancy. I will not.*

Lunchtime

I think it went well. Okay... it could've gone better. It's a bit strange being interviewed by people you already work with. I had to rush out of the interview room once because I felt so sick. They were nice to me, though. They said I looked really poorly and that I should've called in sick if I wasn't feeling well.

'You don't have to be a hero!' one quipped. I tried to smile at him. But I don't think it came out that way, more like a scowl.

Amanda hardly said a word during the interview. Did she suspect? Or was she thinking of next week's wedding? I think she's guessed.

I called Mum. I desperately needed to hear her voice.

'I was just about to call you. How are you feeling?' she asked.

'Okay. Don't laugh, but I think I've had a touch of sunstroke.'

'Of course, you did. Happens to Nigerians all the time,' she cooed, unmistakably sarcastic.

What I needed was a coo full of real love.

'Mum, I'm serious.'

'Of course you are, darling. Anyway, have you spoken to Foluke this weekend? Her father called yesterday. He said he was going to order her back to Nigeria if she didn't sort herself out with a job.'

'No, I haven't. I've just been so busy. Why don't you talk to her? You're her favourite aunt.'

'Baby, are you okay? You don't sound yourself.'

I fought back tears. 'I'm okay. Just tired.'

'You tell that Amanda, if she doesn't leave you alone, she'll have to deal with me, okay?'

'Yes, Mother. Got to go. Love you and Dad.'

'Love you, too, Ms Marketing Director.'

I ran to the toilet, where I stayed for some time waiting to feel more like normal. I wasn't my usual soaring-eagle self. I checked my mobile when I got back to my desk. Three missed calls. I knew they were from Zack and Vanessa, wanting to know if I felt better and how the interview went.

Vanessa. I'll talk to Vanessa. She'll listen. She'll pray for me.

I called her and asked her to meet me at my flat after work.

'I have an idea for your wedding but I'm not telling you until I see you,' I said. She wanted to know how my interview went but I cut her off by pretending I was in a rush.

'I'm praying for Amanda and Robert's wedding next week,' she trilled before getting off the phone.

Come tonight, the only prayers she'll be saying will be for me.

Next, I called Zack. I told him I was feeling better and that the interview went well. I also told him to stop fretting. He said he loved me. I told him I loved him too.

I went to the toilet again and looked at my stomach in the mirror. There couldn't possibly be a baby in there. No way. I didn't even look remotely like a mother.

Mother. I pushed the thought away. It was unbearable.

Vanessa. She can help me make sense of this. She'll listen to me and tell me how much God loves me. I can do this.

I called Zack again to tell him I would probably spend the night at my flat as Vanessa and I had to do wedding stuff.

'Don't work too hard. I could come over–'

Ever the hero. Does he ever stop?

'No, it's okay. I won't stay up late, I promise. Go on, splurge. Get a takeaway, fall asleep in your dirty clothes and drool away on the sofa. I promise I won't make a fuss when I come back tomorrow.'

'I'll see you tomorrow. Tell Vanessa I said hi.'

'Will do.'

1am

Vanessa's asleep in my spare room but I can't sleep. I keep on replaying our conversation in my head.

'Go on, tell me the idea,' she squealed, as soon as I opened the front door to her. 'Ooh, I can't wait to hear it!'

'Sit down first,' I said, leading her to the sofa. She sat down, still smiling. I took a deep breath.

'I'm pregnant.'

She looked at my face and knew I wasn't joking.

'Kemi, how could this happen? I thought you, of all people, would be careful?!'

'I didn't want to go on the pill. And Zack and I were careful but I do remember that one time... well, anyway, I didn't think anything was going to happen... Vanessa, help me. I don't know what to do... '

'What do you mean, *you don't know what to do?* You're pregnant. What else is there to do?'

I couldn't answer because I was afraid of what I would say.

'What did Zack say?'

'I haven't told him.'

'Why not?'

'Because I only found out yesterday.'

'So when are you going to tell him?'

'What makes you so sure I'm going to tell him?'

'Kemi Smith, you're starting to make me feel very nervous. What are you saying?'

My mobile rang. It was Dad. He wanted to check I was okay.

Mum told him I didn't sound well when she spoke to me earlier, he said. I told him I was fine, a bit harassed, what with the interview, the campaign and trying to help out with Vanessa's wedding plans etc.

The phone rang again as soon as I chased him off.

'Are you sure you're okay?' It was Dad again.

'Of course! Stop worrying! Vanessa's here and we have so much to do. I'll call you tomorrow. Bye!'

Vanessa had left the room. She came back from the kitchen with two mugs of tea and handed me one.

'I didn't mean for this to happen,' I said.

Vanessa took the mug from my hand, set it on the floor and hugged me tightly. We both sniffed a bit. I told her I didn't want the baby. She stiffened and withdrew from me.

'You tell me right now what you're saying!'

'I'm saying that I don't want to be pregnant. I'm saying that I don't want to have this baby. This thing that's in me and growing in me and holding me prisoner against my will! I don't want it!' Tears coursed down my cheeks.

'I need to be sure I understand what you're saying. Look me in the eye and tell me!'

'Just leave me alone!'

I ran to the bathroom and grabbed some toilet roll. I ran through the living room and into the bedroom. Vanessa followed me and we both sat on the floor leaning back against the bed. She didn't say anything. We didn't speak for about half an hour. Too busy weeping. Each for different reasons.

'You have to tell Zack–'

'I don't have to tell anyone anything.'

'I'm glad you told *me*.'

'You're my best friend. You drive me nuts, but I don't have anyone else.'

'Kemi, what's going to happen?'

'I don't know,' I yawned. 'I'm just so tired.'

Vanessa got up. 'I'll just go and get my bed sorted and then, tomorrow, we'll figure something out.'

'Vanessa?'

'Yes?'

'Please don't hate me.'

'Never.'

I undressed and sank under the duvet gratefully. I left the door slightly open. I could hear Vanessa praying in the spare room.

That was two hours ago. My body is tired but my mind is too active. I can't sleep. My mind raced from Zack to my parents to Vanessa to Pastor Michael to Foluke to the Sanctifieds. What would they say? What would people say at work? I'd managed to keep my relationship with Zack very much a none-of-your-business thing – but a pregnancy? I pictured Sharronne saying 'I always knew she was a hypocrite. And you all thought she was so holy!'

I mustn't let Zack know about this pregnancy.

Tuesday July 31

The world is firmly established; it cannot be moved (Psalm 93:1).

Vanessa called in sick for me this morning. I also called Zack to let him know I wasn't going to work because I still felt poorly... which wasn't a lie because I did feel poorly. Except I'm not poorly. I'm pregnant.

Vanessa popped out to get some food for breakfast. Like I wanted to eat. The thought of food sickened me.

Then the doorbell rang. It was Zack.

'There's something you're not telling me,' he said, as soon as he came in. 'What is it?'

I told him I was fine. A bit poorly, yes, but fine. I asked him why he wasn't at work, turning my face away from him so he wouldn't see my eyes were red.

'Don't change the subject and stop trying to hide your face from me. Something's happened and you don't want to tell me. Where's Vanessa? Vanessa!' he shouted, storming into the kitchen.

'She's not here! Stop shouting!'

'You're running away from me. We've been here before. I know the signs. Something's happened–'

'Stop saying that! Nothing... absolutely nothing's happened. Stop worrying. Vanessa's just gone to get some bread and milk. So you can go to work now.'

Zack leaned against the kitchen sink and folded his arms. 'I'm not going anywhere. I'm going to wait until Vanessa gets here and I get some answers.'

'Fine. Suit yourself.' I left him in the kitchen and went into the bedroom. He followed me. I ignored him and curled up in bed in the foetal position. He made as if to caress my hair and I shrank from him.

'Kemi, talk to me. What's wrong?'

I didn't answer. Eventually he left me alone and went back to the kitchen. A few minutes later, I heard Vanessa opening the front door. She knew Zack was here. His car was parked right outside my flat.

'Kemi?' she called out, tentatively.

'Vanessa?' Zack called out, half-angry, half-nervous. Two of the most important people in my life and all I've ever done is cause them strife.

I made up my mind not to leave my bedroom.

There was a knock on the half-open door and Vanessa came into the bedroom, followed by Zack.

'Kemi, you can't run away from this forever. Please, just talk to Zack.'

I ignored her.

'Fine. I'll do it. I'll tell him. Zack, Kemi's—'

'SHUT UP! JUST SHUT UP!' I screamed.

Zack looked from me to Vanessa and back to me. He moved closer to the bed. I jumped up and made as if to walk out of the room. Zack blocked me, grabbed my arm and said, 'You're pregnant—'

Vanessa left us alone.

'—and you weren't going to tell me, were you?'

I sat down on the bed. 'No.'

Zack moved closer and tried to put his arm round me.

'Don't touch me!'

It was all his fault. I was fine. Doing okay in church, trying to serve God. But Zack had to come and hover around me like a lovesick puppy and be the perfect son to my parents. I had compromised my faith for him and what did I get in return? This. A baby. A little body of cells threatening to hold me captive against my will. Forever.

'Kemi, don't you want kids?'

'Not like this.'

Not outside of marriage, with someone who doesn't share my faith and certainly not now. I'm 28; just a child myself. What did I know about being a mother? What would everyone say? I pictured myself with a bumpy tummy, everyone staring at me. I winced. No way would I let that happen.

'We can make it work–'

'I'm not having this baby, Zack.'

'What do you mean?'

'I'm telling you that I don't want this baby.'

'No... you don't mean that. You're tired... '

'I'M NOT HAVING THIS BABY!'

He left me alone, went into the kitchen to talk to Vanessa. The tears came again. I made no move to stop them.

Some time later I heard him leave, telling Vanessa he'd be back. Still later I heard the low sound of Vanessa muttering in prayer in the spare room. Dear predictable, comforting Vanessa.

'Vanessa?'

She hurried into my room.

'What are you praying about?'

She said she was praying that I would experience the renewed love of God in my life, eat the food she's about to make and, last but not least, get some sleep.

'A tall order but I think he's answered one of your prayers already. I think I might want to eat.'

'I'll call you when the food's ready.'

'Vanessa, do you think I'm a bad person?'

'You're made in God's image and he doesn't make mistakes.'

'I don't want this baby, Vanessa.'

'Just rest while I'm cooking.'

I fell asleep as soon as she left my room. That's two of her prayers answered, I thought when she woke me nearly an hour later to tell me the chicken and rice was ready.

Afterwards she made me go straight back to bed again. When I next woke, Zack was sitting on a chair near the bed.

'We need to talk,' he said.

'So... you start.'

He started by saying he loved me and that he had never regretted being with me and meeting my parents. Like that mattered right then. I told him I still didn't want the baby. But he didn't get it.

'Why? Explain to me. I thought you would want to have my kids, that this would be what we both wanted.'

'Yes, but not like this. How can I have a child outside of marriage? And I'm not ready to be a mother yet... What will everyone say? What about my job, my career? My parents?'

'I asked you to marry me–'

'I can't marry you. You're not a Christian–'

'I've never stopped you going to church. You chose to stop going yourself.'

He didn't understand.

'It's more than going to church. It's something else. It's about Jesus... '

'Whatever it is, I've never stopped you from doing it.'

I began to cry again. 'You're right. You didn't. I did it myself.'

Zack never could bear to see me cry. He took out a tissue and started wiping my face and kissing me.

'Kemi, we can do this. Please, I'll do anything you want me to do but think about what you're saying... '

'I have thought about it.'

'You know I've been down this road before. I can't let it happen again. I won't let it.'

I hated what I was doing to him but it was my decision to

make, not his. And I hated the way he was comparing me to *her* and I told him as much.

'But you are behaving exactly like she did and saying all the things she said. She killed my baby without telling me and that's what you're planning to do. I cannot let this happen to me again. I *will not* let it happen.'

'I'm not killing anything – and stop comparing me to her. I'm not like her!'

'But you are! And you can call it what you like: termination, abortion, pro-choice – but the end result is still the same: murder!'

I slapped him. His face hardened.

'If you try to do this thing you're planning, I will take you to court and I will win. You know I will. It might be your body, but that's also my child.' And he left the flat, slamming the door behind him.

Vanessa ran in when she heard the front door slam. But I turned my back to her and after a few minutes she left too.

Friday August 3

In that day I will restore David's fallen tent. I will repair its broken places, restore its ruins, and build it as it used to be (Amos 9:11).

Back at work. I had to come in. The Singing Diapers Star Babies campaign has to go on regardless of the disaster otherwise known as my life. Zack hasn't called me and I can't face my parents. What would I say? *Mum, Dad, I'm pregnant! Bring out the fizz!* Gag! I can't even imagine the disappointment on Dad's face. My parents don't even know that I've kind of moved in with Zack. And children outside of marriage? Yeah, right. They would kill Zack and me, then kill themselves straight after. I can't tell them. What if I give Mum another stroke?

I shouldn't have come in today. I can't concentrate and James isn't in. The LPO conductor just called to talk about ideas for the Star Babies single and I really messed up.

'Classical music: Bach, Handel, Haydn, you choose,' I told him at first and then remembered that the research focus groups chose Mozart above all other composers for baby music. I had to call him back.

Amanda came over to my desk and she wasn't winking.

'Don't forget: Roseberry Avenue, next Tuesday, eleven o'clock. Great work on Singing Diapers. Just got the figures. An amazing 25,000 babies auditioned nationally. Good work!'

Babies. That word again.

This morning at the flat I thanked Vanessa for all she'd done for me over the last couple of days and told her I needed to be alone. She made me promise her that I wouldn't go anywhere or do anything without telling her. She also asked me if I wanted to talk to Pastor Michael. I said no. What good would talking do?

'You can always talk to God,' she said as we waited for the bus together. 'There was a time when all you did was talk about and to him. You can still do that. The barriers between you and him are purely of your own making. Not his.'

'You said you wouldn't preach.'

'God's arms are not so short he cannot pull us back from wherever we are. Remember that.'

'Whatever.'

Later

I realised during the afternoon that I had to go to Zack's. I hoped he wouldn't be there. I didn't want a scene. I just wanted to pick up my stuff, go home and think some more.

But he was home when I got there after work. I ignored him and started picking up my things. When I got to the front door with my bags, he ran down the stairs, put his hand on the door handle and said I wasn't going anywhere until we'd sorted things out.

I could've made a scene but I didn't want to. I'd hurt him enough already. In fact, it seemed all he'd ever known with me was pain. I couldn't think of one occasion when he'd ever hurt me knowingly. He would rather die than do something like that. *Zack, my brick. What have I done to you?*

He picked up my bags and started walking up the stairs. He

dropped the bags inside the living room and gestured to the sofa. We both sat down. I apologised for slapping him. He shrugged. I told him I didn't want to talk. Then he said he'd called my parents to come over because they had a right to know what was happening.

'You have no right–'

'You didn't leave me any choice and this affects us all.'

Suddenly, I was tired of the whole thing. Fine, let them come. He can tell them how he got their only daughter pregnant. Let's see how you handle this, Mr Perfect!

They arrived looking very apprehensive. Zack gave them the news straight. At first they took it quite well, even Dad. I thought he would be livid but he wasn't.

'This is the way the world is now,' he said.

Mum went into overdrive.

'It just means you'll speed up your wedding, of course. That's where you were headed anyway. I would've liked things to be done properly but I guess it's a bit late for that now.'

I refused to look at Zack.

'She won't marry me.'

My parents looked at me, questions on their faces.

'Kemi won't marry me because I'm not a Christian, and she doesn't want my baby because she doesn't want a child outside marriage and because she's not ready to be a mother and because it's not the right time.'

'But I thought you wanted to marry Zack!' Dad spluttered.

'Forget Zack!' Mum hollered. 'What do you mean... *she doesn't want my baby?*'

Zack didn't reply. He looked at me. *Go on, tell them,* his eyes challenged me.

I looked away from all of them.

'I'm talking to you, Kemi. Answer me, right this minute!' Mum commanded.

'Stop shouting at her! She's not deaf!' Dad hollered back at her and then turned to me.

'Kemi, talk to us. What is going on?'

The tears started.

'Crying won't solve this. I suggest you start talking some sense,' Mum said.

Dad shot her a venomous look. She drew in a deep breath.

'Maybe Zack will enlighten us,' Mum said, turning to Zack.

I wasn't going to let Zack speak for me. I told them I was indeed pregnant. Yes, Zack proposed and yes, I refused to marry him because he wasn't a Christian.

'So why are you together if you're not going anywhere with this relationship? Surely, it's not because of us?!' Dad was quite upset.

'The baby, Kemi, the baby. What's all this talk about you not wanting the baby?'

Mum was relentless.

'I can't have this child. I'm not ready to be a mother.'

'Don't be silly. I was only 18 when I had you... '

'That's different. You had Dad–'

'And you have Zack. What's the problem?'

'It's not the right time... '

Mum got up. 'You're having this child and that's that. I'm going to go home with your father and tomorrow we're going to talk about this when everyone is in a better frame of mind.'

'She doesn't have to do anything she doesn't want to do. She's 28,' Dad countered.

'I don't care if she's 60; she's still having this child.'

'You can't force her.'

'Watch me.'

I escaped to the bathroom. I couldn't bear to see my parents argue because of me. There was a knock on the door and Zack came in.

'I'm sorry,' he said.

'Not half as sorry as I am. Hope you're happy. This was what you wanted, wasn't it?'

'No, I want you. I want the baby. I want us.'

I blew my nose. It seemed that everybody wanted the baby

but no one was thinking about me. What about my life, what I want?

'You shouldn't have called them.'

'I know. I panicked.'

I blew my nose again and brushed past him into the living room. My parents were still arguing. By the time they left, they weren't speaking to one another. Later Mum texted me to say she would speak to me tomorrow. Dad called my mobile and left a message: 'Talk to Zack. You need to sort this out between the two of you. Don't worry about your mother. We survived the Atlantic. We'll survive this. I love you.'

Tears welled up in my eyes.

Zack wouldn't let me go back to my flat and I was too worn out to argue. Later, in the kitchen, he tried to hug me but I shrank away from him. I didn't want him touching me. What does he know? I'm the one that has to deal with this, not him. We stood in the kitchen staring at each other.

Then he started.

'Kemi, please, I'm begging you. Don't hurt my baby. I don't think I can deal with this a second time. We'll manage. I promise we'll be okay. I'll do whatever you want me to do, but let my child live.' Then we both started crying like fools. This wasn't meant to happen. God, how did I get here?

Saturday August 4

If you then, though you are evil, know how to give good gifts to your children, how much more will your Father in heaven give the Holy Spirit to those who ask him! (Luke 11:13).

Back in my flat. I called a cab at 2am to take me home. I couldn't stay at Zack's. I had to get away. Last night, after we both cried in the kitchen, he got on his *knees* and *begged* me not to kill his baby. I hated seeing him like that. That wasn't my Zack. Crying and begging me like some pathetic, snivelling creature. My Zack is a brick; unmovable and unshakable. Built to last and to withstand the fiercest battering. Even Hurricane Kemi. He got me so angry. 'I'm not a murderer!' I screamed at him. *'Why do I have to be stuck with something I don't want?'*

It's clear to me now: I should never have gone to Zack's office on that day. That was my biggest mistake. I should've let him go. But I didn't because I thought he was mine to do as I wanted. He deserves better.

My eyes hurt. I've been crying non-stop for almost a week. I wish I could rewind the tape of my life. All I'd ever thought about was my desires. I wanted Zack and I didn't care how I got him. And now, *this.*

My devotional verse for the day didn't make me feel better. At all. My parents will be here soon.

'Just the three of us. We'll talk about this like a proper family,' Mum said on the phone.

I just want to crawl under my duvet and forget about the whole world.

Later

But it was Zack who rang the doorbell next.

'Zack, I'm tired and my parents will be here in a minute. Please leave.'

He stood in the doorway for what seemed like forever, just looking at me.

'Kemi, I didn't come after you. You chose to be with me. You chose not to marry me. You chose not to do your church stuff. So why are you punishing me?'

I ignored him.

'Move in with me and I promise I will never ask you to marry me. We'll have the baby and everything will work out fine. Even your parents. They'll come round. You'll see... '

I tried to tell him it wasn't the time to talk about this. He wasn't listening. He said he would get an injunction against me if I went ahead with a termination. Then he started apologising and telling me how sorry he was and that he loved me. Then he left and I called Vanessa.

'Kemi, you know how I feel about this, so why are you calling me? You know what you're proposing is not right.'

I really wanted Vanessa to understand.

'I can't be a mother. I'm not ready. Not now. I've got so much going on–'

'You mean it's a rather *inconvenient* time to have a baby?'

I wished she hadn't put it like that.

'It's just... it's just... nothing's going the way I thought it would go. Zack... he's the only man I've ever wanted but he's not a Christian–'

'Does that matter now? You're pregnant. Let's deal with the real issue. Forget about the 'Christian' stuff. The real reason you don't want to marry him is because you feel condemned and are trying to negotiate your faith and you don't want this child because you think it will be a reminder of how far you've strayed from God.'

She didn't understand.

'Kemi, I do understand. A lot more than you think I do.'

'I'm not ready to be a mother. This wasn't meant to happen. Zack and I were meant to be more settled–'

'You wouldn't marry him so why did you think your relationship had a future?'

'Something would've worked out. We just needed more time.'

'Kemi, babies are a gift from God. Don't do something you'll regret for the rest of your life.'

'I don't want anyone to look at me and mock me. *Look! There goes the fallen saint. Oh look! Another single black mother. She left the church and now she's pregnant.* I couldn't bear it. At least, this way, no one would ever know.'

'The church is made up of imperfect people just like you. You should know that or have you forgotten? At least speak with Pastor Michael. You have so much going for you: friends and family who love you and support you. Once you cross this line, you can never go back. Never.'

'It will go to heaven.'

'Not good enough, Kemi. God has a plan for your child on earth.'

'Don't bring God and his plans into this. I chose Zack over him, so that's it. I don't want this pregnancy. And you can't stop me!'

By this point I was verging on hysteria, and she was getting more and more concerned. But the doorbell rang and put an end to the call. Can't face writing any more today.

Sunday August 5

Be careful not to do your 'acts of righteousness' before men, to be seen by them. If you do, you will have no reward from your Father in heaven (Matthew 6:1).

The rest of yesterday did not go any better.

Dad said I should do whatever made me happy and Mum said I ought not to be so selfish. She asked what I would do if the operation was a disaster and I couldn't have kids ever, and what about Zack? Didn't he have a say in the matter as he had a part to play in it as well? I told her it was my choice to make. She said it wasn't, because it was also their grandchild we were talking about or had I forgotten? And had Dad forgotten that? Then, they started screaming and yelling at each other. Mum wouldn't leave. Said I needed someone to talk some sense into me, and that I looked awful and needed taking care of. Dad found out she'd packed an overnight bag and hidden it in the boot. He was furious. He said it was my life and that I was old enough to make decisions myself, and no one should interfere. Mum said he could do and say whatever he wanted but she wasn't going home with him. She would stay with me until tomorrow or whenever I saw sense.

I spent the rest of yesterday in my bedroom, and Mum and I haven't spoken today. She made me breakfast, forced me to eat it, then just sat down staring at the wall. I left the flat when she went to the bathroom. I figured a ride on a bus to ANYWHERE was better than being in my flat with my mother.

So here I am. On a bus. Going NOWHERE and ANYWHERE. Much like my life.

Later – in a park

I spotted my bus-stop friend the minute he got on the bus. I looked for somewhere to hide, but I was wedged between an oversized Nigerian and his equally oversized wife. Suddenly the littered floor of the bus metamorphosed into a brilliant work of art and I examined it for dear life.

Like that would stop him? What is it with people? You have one conversation with them – a random one I might add – and it's like you're best friends for life. From the corner of my eye, I saw him approach me. I refused to look up and then I heard him.

'Hello! I'm so glad to see you again. I've been praying that I would run into you some day.'

I looked up and gave him a blinding Colgate smile. Even when he settled himself in the seat opposite me, I didn't stop smiling, although my jaw hurt.

'Praise God!'

He couldn't have said it any louder with a microphone. The Oversizeds nodded their approval. The rest of the passengers looked at us briefly and went back to their business. My smile wattage decreased as I furiously tried pretending that all this was normal, but that I wasn't really with the guy. I was just being polite. I looked out of the window. But he was unstoppable.

'Thanks to your words to me that day, I started attending church and am now born again—'

I didn't wait to hear the rest. We were just slowing for a bus stop. I legged it. As in: I hurled myself from between the Oversizeds and ran for it. So he got saved. Big deal. Well, I've just found out I'm pregnant and I don't want to be. Beat that.

What am I saying?!

Monday August 6

Rejoice greatly, O Daughter of Zion! Shout, Daughter of Jerusalem! See, your king comes to you, righteous and having salvation, gentle and riding on a donkey, on a colt, the foal of a donkey (Zechariah 9:9).

Lord, I'm sorry. I'm glad my bus-stop friend got saved. I guess I felt jealous because he just seemed so happy and so secure. I miss that feeling.

I stayed away from my flat all day yesterday. In the end I took the bus to central London and got on one of those tour buses. It was better than being alone with Mum, wondering when and how she'd clobber me. I didn't want to think. When I got back to my flat in the evening, Mum had left. She left me a note. She said she loved me and she'd never regretted having me and, next to meeting my father, having me was the best thing in her life. Could I at least think about my decision one more time?

I didn't call her back. I crawled under my duvet, but I was unable to sleep. I missed Zack. What was he doing?

Maybe I could do it. Maybe I could be a mother.

No. Dirty nappies, sleepless nights, no life, no career. An endless round of snotty noses and pushing prams in the park while Zack worked in his fancy office in the city.

This was your Technicolor dream.

No, it wasn't meant to happen like this. It was meant to have a happy ending and we would have got there if God hadn't done this to me.

Lord, I'm sorry. Forgive me. *Zack, my brick. Where are you?*

Got myself to work somehow. James is beside himself today about Star Babies. He's just spoken to the LPO conductor. Now he's decided he's an *aficionado* of classical music. If he plays that Mozart CD one more time, I'll decapitate him.

The media coverage for the competition has been gathering momentum. It's been great actually. I should be happy but I'm not. I feel dead inside.

I must call Zack. Last night I woke up in the middle of the night expecting to find him next to me. He was far away, in his flat. With Maxine?

He wouldn't do that.

Amanda is not in the office today but she's left me an internal memo with a smiley emoticon: *Tomorrow is the big day!*

No one has called me yet today. Not my parents, not Vanessa and not Zack. I wish they would. I desperately need someone to talk to.

You can always talk to me.

I closed my ears to the Voice. I didn't want to hear him. He was the cause of all my trouble.

I didn't eat breakfast this morning. I've decided to stop eating. Maybe this thing inside me will go away into nothingness if I don't feed it.

Later

I couldn't resist. I had to call Zack.

'Do you hate me?'

'Never.'

Tears welled up in my eyes. He didn't hate me.

'Can I come to yours after work?' I asked him, holding my breath.

Zack sighed. 'Kemi, we can't go on like this. I've tried very hard to please you and do everything on your terms but, honestly, I don't know what else to do. You're squeezing the life out of me.'

'I just want to be with you.'

He was silent.

'What about tomorrow's wedding?' I asked.

'I'll be there.'

I made an excuse about still feeling poorly and left the office early. James could do without me; he was humming away to Handel when I left. I made my way to Zack's flat and let myself in. Then I waited. When I heard him turn the key, I pulled the door open from the inside and wrapped my arms tightly around his neck. He didn't push me away.

'I'm so sorry Zack. I really am.'

I spent the night.

Tuesday August 7

Do not make idols or set up an image or a sacred stone for yourselves, and do not place a carved stone in your land to bow down before it. I am the LORD your God (Leviticus 26:1).

This morning, I opened my eyes to find Zack looking at me. He pushed my hair out of my eyes.

'Have the baby and give it to me. I won't trouble you ever again. Just have the baby.'

I turned my face away. 'No.'

'Have the baby and don't look back.'

'Can't you see that once it's born, I won't be able to give it away? I'll be trapped–'

'You will be the mother of my child, our child. Is that so bad?'

'I'll be stuck at home, with no life and no career. You'll be out working, having fun.'

'Fine, I'll leave my job. I'll stay home. Anything, just don't do this.'

Was he crazy?

'Don't be stupid,' I muttered irritably. Did he think it was that easy? Even my Technicolor dream didn't allow for such fantasies.

'What else do you want me to do? I'm running out of options here.' He pushed back the duvet and rolled out of bed. We both got ready for Amanda and Robert's wedding.

Just before we left, I saw him look at my daily Bible devotional book next to my journal.

'What's that?' he asked. 'Is that the stuff you read every morning?'

'Yes, what about it?'

'Nothing.'

The wedding went well, if a bit brisk. Robert and Amanda looked happy. Zack and I signed as witnesses.

'What now?' Zack asked the newly-weds.

'Well, you two go back to work – and we head off to Spain! Robert and I handed in our resignations this morning. We bought a wine bar in Madrid last month. We've no plans to come back to London.'

Robert put his hand on Amanda's elbow. 'Come on, we've got a plane to catch. Thanks for coming, guys. We really appreciate it.'

Zack and I couldn't speak. We followed them out of the registry office and watched them get into a black cab and drive away. Amanda waved. I waved back. My throat constricted. *She got her dream.*

My mobile rang. It was James.

'Have you heard the news? Amanda and Robert resigned this morning! Sharronne told me they were getting married. Is that true?'

'James, I can't talk right now. I'll call you back.'

Zack waited on the pavement.

'Where do we go from here, Kemi?'

'I don't know.' Actually, I did know but I wasn't going to tell him. I was done with discussions, arguments and pleadings. It was time for action. It was time I took control of my life.

I didn't go back to work. The place would be in uproar. I jumped off the tube when it reached my stop, without a backward glance at Zack. When I got home, I dialled the number I'd found in Yellow Pages.

'Choice,' the woman on the other end said.

'Yes, I would like to make an appointment please.'

Afterwards I took a couple of sleeping pills and slept. I hadn't eaten for almost two days.

Wednesday August 8

The Lord has dealt with me according to my righteousness; according to the cleanness of my hands he has rewarded me (2 Samuel 22:21).

Absolute pandemonium at work today. I didn't get home until 10pm. I can't believe Amanda's left me in the lurch like this. She's in Madrid living her Technicolor dream and I'm picking up the pieces. Apparently she and Robert booked their annual leave, all 25 days of it, like two months ago and took it as the 25 days' formal notice the company requires.

I don't really blame her. If I had the guts, I would've done the same. And guess who's stuck with Amanda's work until a replacement is found? Yes, moi! And, oh yes, James told me on the sly, 'Just so you know, Sharronne is going to bid for your old job once you get the Marketing Director's post. Talk about happily ever after.' And he grinned.

Mum called late morning.

'Have the baby and give it to us. We'll bring it up as ours and you don't have to have anything to do with it. Ever.'

'I can't talk about this now, Mum.'

'Fine. We'll talk some more when you get home. I love you.'

I didn't reply and it hurt her. I felt it in the silence after her declaration.

'All that time you were going to church… and you decide to do this. Why? Is life of such little value to you that you decide to take matters into your own hands because you don't want to be inconvenienced?'

'Drop it, Mum.'

'I'm just trying to make you see… ' her voice faltered. She was weeping. 'My child, I love you so much… but this is wrong. Promise me you won't do anything until we've talked about this some more.'

Once again, I was silent.

'Kemi, I said, *Promise me.*'

'I'm not promising anything to anyone. I just want to be left alone.'

'Kemi… you haven't made an appointment or anything, have you? Dear God! Kemi, listen to me–'

'I'm sorry, Mother, but I have to go.'

I hurried to the toilet, threw up, rinsed my mouth and splashed cold water on my face. I felt weak. I hadn't eaten since Mum forced me to have breakfast on Sunday morning, three days ago. I wished my tummy was empty, but it wasn't. I have something inside me that keeps on growing despite my best efforts to neutralise it.

Is there a way back?

How can I go back to church when I still love Zack and want to be with him? I tried to give him up and it almost killed me.

No, once the pregnancy's gone I can make everything right with Zack. Zack is just not thinking strategically about our careers or anything. We can start again, maybe sort out the Jesus/faith/church issue, get settled in our careers and, maybe, even marry. *Then* we'll start breeding.

Saturday August 11

Many are the plans in a man's heart, but it is the LORD's purpose that prevails (Proverbs 19:21).

Saturday. I'm a prisoner in my own flat. A few hours after my last journal entry I fainted in the office toilet. Sharronne found me and called an ambulance. As if that wasn't bad enough, she was nominated to go in the ambulance with me. So humiliating.

I regained consciousness in the ambulance to find Sharronne flirting with a paramedic. When she realised I was awake, she lowered her eyes.

'How are you feeling?' she asked. If I didn't know better, I would think she cared.

'She'll be alright,' said the paramedic, cheerily.

He leaned over me.

'You need a break, that's all. Probably been overworking and your body's telling you to slow down. I see it all the time. You young career girls.'

My parents were waiting at the hospital entrance.

'We didn't know what to do. Someone got their number from HR,' Sharronne explained.

The paramedics lowered me into a wheelchair waiting on the tarmac. My parents rushed towards me.

'What happened? My God, are you okay? Is it the baby?'

Not for the first time in my life, I wished I had the guts to tell Mum where to stick her mouth. From the corner of my eye, I saw Sharronne's eyes widen in shock. I resolutely refused to look at her.

'Are you the one that found her in the loo?' Dad asked.

Sharronne nodded.

'Thank you very much. Kemi, are you alright? We've been so worried!'

'I'm fine. Just tired, that's all.'

'Of course, you're tired! You're pregnant!' Mum snapped.

Dad waded in. 'The girl was unconscious and all you can think about is the fact that she's pregnant. What about her?'

'Dad, it's okay.'

'No, it's not okay. I told your mother to let sleeping dogs lie but–'

Mum turned to Sharronne. She thanked her for coming with me and asked her to keep everything she'd heard to herself.

Sharronne nodded.

I was out of the hospital within the hour. The doctor told Mum I needed taking care of as he could see I hadn't eaten for some time. Nothing new, he said. Evidently, lots of women with 'compromising' pregnancies choose starvation as an easy termination 'mechanism'. Mum was livid.

'I can't believe you were thinking of starving your own child to death! Too far. You have gone too far! Kemi Smith, what is wrong with you?'

Dad was sombre. I think he was frightened of what was happening to me. When they brought me home, he laid me on the bed and just held me. I could tell he was trying to hold back his tears because his body was shaking.

'I'm so sorry, Dad.'

'It's alright, baby. Hush, don't cry. You'll be okay. We'll figure something out.'

Later that night, I heard him talking to Mum in the spare room.

'Gail, she hadn't eaten for days. Days! What if she had been in her flat alone when she fainted? It stops here and now. Leave her alone. Let her do what she wants.'

'But it's wrong, Femi. It's wrong.'

'Well, I would rather have my daughter than a corpse, and that is exactly what we will have if you don't lay off. She was *starving* herself. You heard the doctor. He knew what she was doing the minute he examined her.'

'But what about Zack? Okay, he's the one that got her into this mess. But doesn't he have a say? It will kill him. You know it will.' Mum was crying.

So here I am back in my flat. I'm mad at myself for missing my appointment at the clinic. My parents have moved in temporarily and it was Mum who picked up the phone when the clinic called about the missed appointment. When she realised who was calling, she gave the poor receptionist an earful and slammed the phone down on her. And, of course, Zack's been here. He's been here every day since I got back from the hospital. We haven't really talked much. He just comes into my bedroom and sits on the chair while I turn my back to him on the bed. Most times, I just look at the wall and refuse to talk to anybody.

Vanessa came yesterday with Pastor Michael and his wife Janice.

'He insisted on coming,' Vanessa said.

I think I was pleased they came. They both held me very tight and let me cry. I didn't say much but that was okay. I don't know why but I felt a lot calmer after their visit.

Dad is going back home tomorrow. He needs to get back to work. Mum and Vanessa will stay with me.

I got the Marketing Director position. The office called me yesterday. They also sent me a get-well card and flowers.

James says the production company have whittled the auditioned babies down to 50. No mean feat considering we had 25,000 applicants. We're on track for the final ten auditions to start broadcasting live on TV in September.

Amanda sent me a text from Madrid. *Sorry 2 dump u in it. Luv Madrid! xxxxxx.*

Foluke came round. Mum told her about the pregnancy.

And still this thing inside me keeps growing.

Sunday August 12

What we are is plain to God, and I hope it is also plain to your conscience (2 Corinthians 5:11).

I was out of bed at the crack of dawn. The flat felt more and more like a prison. Everyone's holding me hostage in case I decide to make another appointment at the clinic.

I was really quiet, creeping about, getting dressed. I opened the front door as quietly as I could. And there he was, Zack, just getting out of his car. I ignored him and started walking. He followed me.

I hadn't really spoken to him for days.

He put his hand on my arm.

'You gave me a real fright, going to hospital.'

I jerked away from him and carried on walking.

'Do you hate me that much that you would try to starve yourself and our baby to death?'

Our baby. That really annoyed me.

'First of all, it's not our baby. Secondly, I'm really sick and tired of everyone calling it a baby. It's not anything. Just some DNA and a bunch of cells or whatever. And, thirdly, I don't hate you.'

He put his hand on my arm again and tried to block my path. I struggled to free myself.

'If you don't let me go, I'll scream.'

'This is London. No one will come. I need you to talk to me.'

I struggled to get free but then gave up.

'Fine. We'll talk.'

He released me and I headed for the park, Zack following. We'd spent many, many hours in that park before. Talking, making plans, being a couple.

We sat on opposite ends of our favourite bench. The park was empty, except for a couple of pensioners walking an ugly spaniel.

'Why are you here, anyway? It's 6.30 in the morning.'

'I wanted to make sure you were okay.'

'Why wouldn't I be? My mother and best friend are holding me hostage in my own flat and you're stalking me.'

Zack tried to hold my hand. I withdrew it.

'There was a time when I couldn't touch you enough.'

'Touching me brought us to this situation.'

He asked me if he could see my belly. Of course, I refused. Then I relented. He was my Zack. I lifted up my t-shirt briefly. Zack put his hand on my stomach, and then he kissed it. Tears welled up in my eyes. I stood up quickly.

'That's it. I'm going home. Don't want the guards to worry now, do we?'

I stayed in my bedroom the rest of the day. I didn't talk to anyone except for Dad. He came by and we talked about the weather, Tony Blair and parking attendants. I told him I'm going back to work tomorrow.

'I can't stay here forever. And there's so much to do at the office.' Paramount of which was eliminating Sharronne, feline extraordinaire.

'Promise me you won't do anything without telling me. I'll even drive you to the clinic myself, if you like. Just tell me before you go anywhere or do anything.'

'Promise.' But there was no way I was going to let him drive me to the clinic. Mum would be devastated. I intended to do this myself.

'I'm taking your mother home with me. You need some time to yourself.'

'Thanks.'

'And talk to Zack. That boy is crazy about you.'

'After this fiasco, he won't ever want to talk to me again.'

Mum didn't make a fuss but left quietly with Dad. Zack turned up and Vanessa said she would go to church but come back afterwards and spend the night.

I wandered into the kitchen where Zack was making coffee. The smell made me queasy. I asked him to open the window or, better still, pour the coffee down the sink. He opened the window *and* poured the coffee into the sink.

'Feeling better?' he asked.

'I'm ready to talk now.'

I jumped straight in and all my thinking of the past few days started to come together. I started by telling him how much I loved him and didn't want to hurt him. Then I talked about how when I decided to become a Christian I finished our relationship because a) I no longer believed in sex before marriage and b) he had no interest whatsoever in sharing my faith. I figured we were going in opposite directions and that this Jesus thing was very important to me.

But then I described how it was very difficult to stay away from him. I had missed him and I was frightened of being alone.

'I wish I could explain my Jesus thing to you, but I can't. I know it's real because of what I've experienced. Talking to Vanessa and lots of the other guys at church I came to understand what God wants from us and how he sent Jesus to this earth to be an example of God-centred living and also to die for us, as a sort of payment for all the wrong things we do. From the time I decided to follow Jesus I began to know what it's like to sense the real presence of God. I know what it's like to feel strong because God is with me.

'I know it doesn't make sense to you, but hear me out. I started to love reading the Bible, trying to dig around in it to find out what it meant for me. There were times I would be in a situation and I wouldn't know what to do and a Bible verse would pop into my head which would give me an answer. God was talking to me, helping me with life here on earth. I was happy in church because I had Jesus and he gave me direction.

'Before that, all I wanted was to be with you, marry you and have your kids. When I became a born-again Christian, my horizons expanded. It was like I was a part of something a lot bigger than myself and I so wanted you to be a part of it with me–'

'So it's all my fault.'

'I didn't say that. Zack, please just hear me out.'

'Fine, talk.'

'But I found it too hard to cope with wanting you as well. You seemed to be everywhere and wouldn't leave me alone. I couldn't stay away from you. So I decided I would try to have both you and my faith. I thought we could be happy. But all along I've understood I can't marry you because you are not a Christian. Despite everything I've done – and I know I've really messed up – my faith is still a very important issue for me. It's been difficult to go back to church because it would mean giving you up, not waking up in the morning with you, not being with you. I'm too weak and selfish. I tried it for a year but I can't do it again. I'm too weak. Then, *this* happened.'

'That's our child you're talking about, not some object.'

'Don't keep interrupting. This is your one chance to have this conversation. If you won't listen, I'll walk out and not talk to you about it again.'

Zack turned his face away from me and I carried on.

'The pregnancy was a shock. I wasn't prepared. It's not something we thought would happen now. In the future, yes, but not now. You know the way I was raised. My parents wouldn't stand for a baby outside marriage. Especially Mum. She likes things done "properly". Besides, what would people say? One minute I'm a Jesus fundamentalist and the next I have a hump the size of Mount Kilimanjaro in front of me. Do you know how humiliating that would be? Besides all that, I'm not ready to be a mother. I'm not. I don't feel anything for what's inside me, Zack. Nothing. It has to go.'

'You're lying.'

'What?'

'You're lying about not feeling anything. You felt something when I put my hands on your tummy and kissed it. You felt something. Even if you couldn't bear to face up to it.'

'Haven't you been listening to me?'

'I have – but it doesn't change the fact that what you want to do is murder. You know how another woman killed – yes, killed – my first baby. Don't turn your face away from me. It almost killed *me*. And I won't let it happen again. That's my child you're carrying and I won't be robbed again.'

'What about me? I'm the one that's carrying it.'

'My mother could have killed me when she found out she was pregnant. But at least she carried me to term. It wasn't convenient for her, but she saw it through.'

'I'm not your mother and I'm not that other woman.'

'That *other woman* killed my child without my knowledge. She terminated the baby because she didn't want it. She told me after she'd done it. She didn't even give me a chance to know I was a father. Have you any idea what that does to me still, seven years on? I was there when this baby was being created – or have you forgotten that?'

Zack walked across the room and put his hand on my belly.

'It's a child, Kemi. Our child. And I believe it will live.'

'That's what you think.'

'*What we are is plain to God and I hope it is also plain to your conscience.* That's the verse for today from that Bible thing that you're always reading. I sneaked a look because I thought it would help me make sense of what you're thinking. I don't know who God is but that verse adds up. Have you listened to your conscience?'

'How dare you preach to me? Who do you think you are!'

I fled to my bedroom. But much later he slid into bed with me and I didn't push him away.

The only thing that's keeping me sane is writing down everything that's happening. I spend hours writing. It helps.

Friday August 17

Our sister, may you increase to thousands upon thousands; may your offspring possess the gates of their enemies (Genesis 24:60).

Can't really write much because I'm sick. I've barely been at work the whole week. It's not looking good with the promotion and everything. People are beginning to talk. But I can handle it. I'm an eagle soaring high in the sky. I've made another appointment with the clinic. The earliest date they have is next Monday.

Zack has more or less moved into my flat. He watches me all the time. And Vanessa's gone back to her parents.

'Everything will work out okay. I can sense it in my spirit. God's will for your life will prevail.'

I was a bit snappy, told her that I was in charge of my life and no one would dictate to me how I lived it.

Pastor Michael's been round again. He finally met Zack and – surprise! He liked him and they got on quite well.

'You must think I'm a really bad person,' I said to the pastor.

'Bad? No. I think you've decided on one way and you're determined not to consider that God might have different plans for you.'

'I'm not a *bad* person.'

'We're all sinful people. That's why Jesus came – to rescue us from our sin.'

'I'm not ready to be a mother. People will point their fingers and laugh at me: the fallen saint. I couldn't bear it.'

'Jesus bore the shame of the cross–'

'I'm not Jesus.'

'You're made in God's image, his child.'

'You don't understand–'

'Maybe not, but God does and he's always on your side. Don't do this thing.'

Talking to him was like beating my head against a wall.

Sharronne sent me an e-card. I didn't bother reading it. I deleted it.

Mum's backed off but we're barely talking. Dad calls me every night to make sure I'm okay.

Foluke's going back to Nigeria next week. She met a guy from there on the Internet and she reckons it's the real thing.

Vanessa's wedding is set for December 8. I'm still going to be the maid of honour.

Everyone's getting on with their lives except me. And still I can't stop this thing inside me from growing. Sometimes, I hold my breath for several minutes because I think it will stop the growing, but of course it doesn't. My breasts are tender and my tummy looks like I've eaten too much.

Zack has started reading my Bible devotionals every day now, but I don't let him talk to me about it.

The Sanctifieds called. Would it be okay for them to come round? I said no and hung up. Let them think what they like. I doubt they ever liked me anyway.

Tuesday September 4

All a man's ways seem right to him, but the LORD weighs the heart (Proverbs 21:2).

So much has happened in the last two weeks. I haven'y felt like writing, but here I am now. I've been back at work, slogging away. The Star Babies competition was on TV on Saturday. I didn't watch it (I really, really cannot deal with babies right now) but everyone said it was great. The show's ratings went through the roof. The format was simple. (Let's face it, what can a year-old baby do?) There was a segment on the babies' cooing factor, the little 'cute' things they do and then there were segments of stuff on pregnancies and baby's health. And during the programme breaks there were adverts for Singing Diapers. And the UK loved it. I've just seen the advertising prices for the show slots in light of its first ratings. It's criminal. All that money to sell dreams to people. I'm almost ashamed to be in this industry. There's talk of *Star*

Babies 2 already. Windy CEO is beside himself. His nappies are selling like hot cakes.

Sharronne and I haven't talked about what she heard at the hospital. If anything, she's made a studious attempt to keep out of my way. She actually left a note on my desk: *I've been there before. I understand.* I threw it in the bin. I don't need sympathisers. Least of all, feline ones. But I sent her a quick email thanking her anyway.

I start my new position next Monday. Mum's still not talking to me. Foluke's gone back to Nigeria. She sent me a text the other day: *Love Lagos, never coming bk to UK. In luv!! Will call u. Don't worry, u will be ok.*

Zack is still living in my flat. He thinks he can watch me forever. He sleeps in the spare room. We barely talk to one another.

I can't put off writing about going to the clinic and everything. I asked Vanessa to come with me. I know it wasn't fair to ask her, but I just couldn't face going on my own. At first she refused. Then she agreed because, well, she's Vanessa, Jesus' blood sister, and she never could refuse anyone in need.

I don't know what I expected to find. A huge sign on the building saying: *Abortion Clinic. Welcome*? The building was nondescript. Vanessa and I went past it twice before we realised it was what we were looking for. There were no signs in front. It didn't even have the building number painted anywhere on it. Then Vanessa decided to have a crisis.

'Kemi, please. I don't think I can do this. Let's go back.'

'Fine,' I said, 'I'll go by myself.' I walked up to the door and pressed the bell. Vanessa hesitated then followed me. A middle-aged woman answered the door, smiling.

'How can I help you?'

'We... I have an appointment.'

'Of course.'

Once inside, she directed us to a waiting room that was totally without character. The colours were neutral but not cold. The atmosphere was neither welcoming nor indifferent. It was just like any other commercial premises.

'If you will fill in this form, a doctor will be with you shortly.'

I could see Vanessa looking around rather intently and I wished she wouldn't. Opposite us was a woman in her early forties. Two seats behind her was another woman about the same age as me. A couple were sitting to my right; the woman was weeping and her partner was murmuring in her ear. I wondered what he was telling her. Whatever it was, I'm sure he wasn't forcing her to go ahead with a pregnancy against her will. Unlike Zack.

I wished I hadn't thought of him just then.

I turned my attention to the form. I didn't want to fill it in, it was like leaving a record which people might read later and then hate me. The questions asked stuff like: *When was the last time you had your period? Is this your first time here? Do you have a support system to help you through this? What are your religious beliefs?* And so on. Lots of questions about medical history. I filled it in and waited.

'Kemi Smith?' the nurse called.

Vanessa inhaled sharply.

I turned to her.

'I'll come in with you,' she said.

'I'm afraid you're not allowed to do that,' the nurse said to Vanessa. 'You can wait here or come back later. As this is an initial consultation, she'll probably be in there for about half an hour.'

The consultation was thorough. The woman doctor was very kind. *Did you know you needed two doctors' signatures before having a termination?* No, I didn't. *Have you spoken about this with your partner and does he support you?* Yes, we've spoken and no, he doesn't agree. *Would you like to see a counsellor before the termination?* No, I just want to do it and forget about it. *When was the last time you had your period? What a shame you couldn't have the abortion pill. It would've been a lot easier because it induces miscarriages but it can only be used for pregnancies up to nine weeks. They could do it for you at 12 weeks but they would rather not. Would you like to know of the various procedures available?* No, not really. I just want to get it over and done with. Well, she's not sure but she thinks I'm about 12 or 13 weeks gone *in which case you would have the gentle suction. It takes less than five minutes and you wouldn't need an anaesthetic. No, it's not painful at all. You would experience a little pain but they would give you some painkillers. Of course you can still have children and of course you won't get cancer. People are misinformed about terminated pregnancies which is why it's important to have the right information so every woman can make an informed decision.* What if I was past 12 weeks? *The procedure would take a bit longer but don't worry, you can still go back to work the next day. No one will know. You don't want your family doctor to know either? Don't worry, they'll source an independent one for you and make sure you get another doctor's signature. Would you like to have the scan now so they can know how far gone the pregnancy is?*

I nodded. I had the ultrasound. I was about 12 weeks. I went to the reception and made the procedural appointment for Saturday – five days away.

Done. In five days, I'll be free, I was thinking. Maybe I'll go away after Saturday. Go to the Maldives. No one knew me in the Maldives. Actually, not the Maldives, it's a couples' ghetto. Maybe Brazil. I've always wanted to go to Brazil. No, too crowded. I need somewhere I can go and think. I need peace and quiet. Ireland. I will go to Ireland straight after the procedure. Maybe not Ireland. What about Scotland? There are mountains in Scotland and Zack loves mountains.

Forget about Zack. It's over between you two. After Saturday, he will never speak to you again.

He will. He's my Zack. He loves me.

I blinked my eyes against the tears. My steps faltered as I went back to the reception where I signed the papers and paid my fee: £500. The receptionist told me I could sign and pay the same day as the operation but I insisted. The less time I wasted on the day, the better. I just wanted to walk in, do it, and forget about it.

You'll never forget about it.

I pushed the Voice away and walked outside where Vanessa was waiting for me. We didn't talk to each other on the way back to my flat.

Then, the day before it was all going to happen, I got a letter. It was an injunction preventing me from taking 'counter-reproductive biological action' before the case of *Kariba* v *Smith* was heard in court. That explains why Zack moved out last Wednesday. He tried talking to me before he left, but I just ignored him. His room is bare. There is no trace of him. Nothing. Like he'd never been there. Seven years and it comes to this? A court action against me?

It's Vanessa. She told him about the appointment. She's been calling me non-stop since yesterday but I've ignored her calls. I don't think I will ever talk to her again. I can't believe she would betray me like that – telling Zack about the appointment.

I haven't told my parents about Zack suing me. In fact, I haven't done anything. After reading the injunction, I called in sick at work and just stayed in my flat all day staring at the wall.

I feel so dead inside. Actually, that's a lie. I feel resentful and hateful. Towards God, towards Zack, towards Vanessa and, most especially, towards this growth in my belly that's ruined my life and everyone else's around me. I hate it. Hate it.

Pastor Michael has been leaving messages on my work, home and mobile phones. I haven't called him back. Once, he and Janice both came to my flat but I pretended I wasn't home.

I was supposed to be free by now. I was supposed to go to Scotland to see the mountains, but I cannot because Zack's taken out an injunction against me. What's happening to my life? Why is everything going wrong? All I ever wanted was to be a good Christian and be with Zack, and it's all gone wrong. Why?

Saturday September 8

I will defend this city and save it, for my sake and for the sake of David my servant (2 Kings 19:34).

I've just called Pastor Michael. He said they would come and see me. I thought hard about my daily Bible verse for the first time in forever. It says God will defend his city. Where are you when I need you Lord? You're supposed to defend me but I just keep getting knocked back? Where are you?

Sunday September 9

But small is the gate and narrow the road that leads to life, and only a few find it (Matthew 7:14).

I'm glad the pastors came round yesterday. It was nice to have someone to talk to without feeling judged or condemned. I told them about Zack's court order.

'I didn't even know people could do that,' Janice said.

'Have you taken legal advice?' Pastor Michael asked.

I shook my head. 'I don't even know where to start looking.'

'Have you tried speaking to Zack? Maybe there's a way you can sort this thing amicably,' the pastor offered.

'We've gone past that now.'

'I think you should call your parents. You need your family with you at this time. You can't do this yourself.'

'Pastor, I can't. Mum's not talking to me and this whole issue has caused a rift between my parents. And I don't want to give my Mum another stroke.'

'At least talk to your father.'

So I called Dad and I told him. He and Mum came straight round to my flat. They called Zack and he refused to call off the injunction. Then Dad made a few calls to his friends. He finally got a lawyer. He called the lawyer's mobile and managed to get an appointment for Monday morning. Mum didn't do anything. She sat on the sofa and absolutely refused to look at me. But just seeing them in my flat made me feel happier.

I went to church today. I slipped in halfway through the sermon and sat right at the back. The Sanctifieds were there, as were Vanessa and Mark. He had his arm around her. I remembered what it felt like to have Zack's arms around me and got annoyed with myself. What was I doing? Wasn't it this same Zack that was suing me? I left the service early; the sermon was on the prodigal son.

When I got home, I had two voicemails. One from Dad. Would I call him? The second message was from Zack. I didn't bother listening to it before deleting it.

Tomorrow I'll see the lawyer and she'll tell me what to do.

Better is open rebuke than hidden love (Proverbs 27:5).

Dad came with me to see the solicitor on Monday. Mum wasn't feeling well. Dad didn't say anything but I knew he was concerned about her.

The lawyer was hopeful.

'It's a bit of a strange one, your case,' she said.

No kidding.

'This kind of injunction is something of a rarity. I'm surprised he even got it. It says here that the clinic doctors did not make a full assessment of your emotional and psychological state before booking you for an abortion procedure. Therefore, they were in clear breach of the 1967 Abortion Act. It says that your emotional state is questionable, and that you can't currently make an informed decision regarding a termination. It's signed by a doctor who says you starved yourself when you found out you were pregnant and that you were found unconscious in the office toilet. That means that your psychological state has to be evaluated before you can go ahead with the termination.

'As I say, I'm amazed Zack got this order. It's practically unheard of. But don't worry, I don't really think it's worth the paper it's printed on. It won't get to court. It's *your* body and *your* reproductive right, and absolutely nothing to do with Zack. Even if you were married, you could still have an abortion with or without your husband's consent. Under a legal precedent set in 1978, there are no paternal rights whatsoever under the 1967 Abortion Act. A man cannot prevent his child from being aborted. So relax. This time next week, all this will be a distant memory.'

'So you're telling me that, if my wife was pregnant, she could have a termination without my consent and I would have no say in it, even though we've been married for 30 years?' asked Dad.

The lawyer nodded. 'Many have tried and failed,' she replied firmly.

When we left the solicitor's office, Dad was quiet.

'I'm sorry, Dad.'

He pulled me close to him and kissed my forehead.

'I didn't know that... about the married woman and her rights... doesn't seem... never mind.'

In one week, I will be free to get on with my life.

Saturday September 15

My lover is radiant and ruddy, outstanding among ten thousand (Song of Songs 5:10).

Zack came here last night but I wouldn't let him in. Then he sent me a text message but I deleted it without reading it. Then Mum called. She hadn't spoken to me voluntarily for about a month now.

'I don't know if I ever told you this, but, the day you were born, your father put you in his arms and walked up and down the hospital ward, showing you off to anyone who would care to listen. He said you were the prettiest, smartest baby in the whole world and that you would become the first black prime minister of Britain. Then he said you would be the first African on the moon.'

That sounded like Dad.

Mum sniffed and continued. 'Some people got really shirty with him. I mean, he was a young black lad strutting up and down with a white-looking baby in his arms and saying all these things. Who did he think he was? But your father didn't care. He was a father and he felt ten feet tall. I don't know why we didn't have other children. It wasn't like we didn't want them – that's the way things happened, but this... this thing you're doing... it's going to affect you forever and if I don't try to make you see that, I won't be doing my job as your mother. It will be there in the background and you'll never be free of it. I know because I know many, many women who've taken that decision and are still suffering the consequences. I know what they tell you at the clinic. But, believe me, a million counselling sessions won't erase the fact that you killed your own son or daughter. I'm a mother. I know what it's like to be pregnant. You cannot deny that you feel something for this child you're carrying because it's a part of you.'

Then she started crying. 'Zack reminds me so much of your

father. So strong and so indestructible on the outside, but soft on the inside. That boy loves you. But, if you go ahead with this, you will destroy him. You know I'm telling the truth. Is that what you want?

'After today, I won't talk about this with you anymore. I will leave you alone. But I just had to say it one last time. You shouldn't have got pregnant in the first place. But abortion's something else. But you go and do whatever it is you want to do. I love you and I want you to be happy. But remember, there's always a cost.'

I went for a walk. Mid-September and the days were still warm. But as I got to the park a bit of a breeze sprang up. I shivered and sat down on my favourite bench. Then I took out my daily devotional, re-read my Bible verse for the day and flicked through my journal. So many words. The park grew still. I thought about many things and remembered many more.

Love is patient, love is kind. It does not envy, it does not boast, it is not proud. It is not rude, it is not self-seeking, it is not easily angered, it keeps no record of wrongs. Love does not delight in evil but rejoices with the truth. It always protects, always trusts, always hopes, always perseveres. Love never fails.

I thought about Vanessa, who had never once failed me and always put my needs first, even though she'd hurt me so much by letting Zack know I was at the clinic. I thought about Pastor Michael, who hasn't once asked me to go back to church, neither has he thrown me out of his congregation and never once judged me. If anything, I've been the one doing the judging and bad-mouthing. I thought about my Mum and my Dad and Zack.

And then I began to see myself the way I really was. I was surrounded by people who continually made sacrifices for me and all I could think about was what I wanted. Me. Me. Me.

I put my hand on my tummy and felt the breeze ruffle my hair.

Friday October 5

See, I have engraved you on the palms of my hands (Isaiah 49:16).

It's a while since I wrote and things have moved on.

Sharronne got my old job. We're not exactly friends yet but I've stopped thinking of her as an enemy. I promoted James to Executive Team Member (whatever that means). I had to be inventive. It was the only way to prevent him from scratching Sharronne's eyes out.

Sales of Singing Diapers are still skyrocketing. The Star Babies album is being recorded. It'll be done minus babies and then the winners' gurgles will be digitally added to the album once they're announced in November.

I got a pay rise the size of a skyscraper and Windy CEO is thinking of developing a new line of products on the Singing Diapers theme. I told him I would think about heading the campaign. He reminded me that the reason my company got Singing Diapers was because of me and that he was forced to relegate his marketing person to another product *because of me*. I told him I meant I would definitely head his campaign.

I'm almost five months pregnant. When Windy CEO found out I was pregnant, he sent me a lorryload of baby products.

Zack and I had our first counselling session with Pastor Michael and Janice today. It went well, I think. It was a bit awkward at first but I think we'll get through. He's dropped the court case.

'I didn't think it would get to court anyway, but I was desperate.'

'You hurt me. I was desperate, too.'

'No, you were thinking only of yourself.'

When Pastor Michael signalled it was time for a break, Janice brought us some iced tea.

'How do you feel?' she asked me.

'Tired. Must we go on with this?' I asked, knowing the answer.

We resumed and finished an hour later. I was shattered. Zack offered to drive me home.

'I've been reading those daily Bible verses. I bought my own copy,' he said on the way to my flat. 'There's a lot of truth in them. You okay?'

I wasn't okay. I wasn't sure how I'd react if he got serious about the Bible. He pulled up outside the flat, got out and helped me out of the passenger seat.

'I'm pregnant, not an invalid,' I protested.

'I know. But I want to do this. I *like* doing this.'

He tried to kiss me.

'Not now Zack. There's just too much stuff going on.'

He went home and I read today's Bible verse again. Not because I wanted to but because I knew I needed help to make sense of my life; to help me to live selflessly. Most of all, to help me to love this human being growing inside me. I can do it. I *will* do it. *Love... is not self-seeking... always perseveres.* I have 1 Corinthians 13 committed to memory. I can do this.

Sunday October 28

The body is a unit, though it is made up of many parts; and though all its parts are many, they form one body. So it is with Christ (1 Corinthians 12:12).

Zack went to church today. He turned up at my parents for Sunday lunch afterwards. His relationship with them is on the mend.

Vanessa's parents dropped some stuff off for the baby yesterday. I reassured them they were in first place for godparents. Truly, they have no shame.

Foluke's engaged.

And me? I think I'm alright. Things are slowly getting better. I'm still not going to church. I can't face everybody looking at me and knowing everything that's happened. Sometimes, I feel so numb. It's like I'm watching myself in a dream or something. Then I look at my belly and I think of Zack's mother and I know that whatever happens between Zack and me, I don't any more want to deny him the gift of a child.

I'm taking one day at a time. The temptation to feel overawed by what's happening to my body and my life is always there. I'm afraid that if I succumb to it, I'll do something drastic.

Why do you run from me, beloved?

Because I'm bad. I've hurt people. I even tried to kill my own child by starving it. And I'm too busy resenting my own child to love it. What kind of person am I?

Saturday November 3

As a shepherd looks after his scattered flock when he is with them, so will I look after my sheep (Ezekiel 34:12).

Tonight was the final show for Star Babies. I've worked my socks off, despite everything going on, and months of hard work really paid off. I couldn't go to the studio to watch it live because I've been rather poorly but James and everyone said it was great! I must have received 50 million texts today. Windy CEO's was the first: *Was the LPO great or what?!* I got one from James: *My cousin's daughter's ex-partner's baby is one of the Star Babies!* I vowed to dismember him on getting to the office on Monday.

Zack's just left. He stayed with me last night. He's really taken with the whole pregnancy thing. He keeps on kissing my tummy and has started reading John Donne to 'my son'. We're not sleeping with each other anymore. In fact, our relationship is in no man's land. We have too much emotional and spiritual baggage to sort out before we can decide where our relationship is going. The counselling sessions are great, even if I do feel sometimes that Zack and I are being stripped bare. But it's good. We talk about lots of things: my fear of being alone, God, Jesus and Zack's childhood in the orphanage.

Janice asked Zack one time if he'd ever thought about tracing his parents.

'Where would I start? I don't even know my race. I think I'm mixed race but I'm not sure. I don't have a name or hospital to start my search with. My surname was the last name of the woman that found me outside the orphanage. I don't even know my birthday. The staff at the orphanage guessed I was about 48 hours old when I was dropped outside their front door and that's the date I celebrate. Even if I wanted to start looking, would my mother want to know me? I think I'm half black plus half Mediterranean or half Middle Eastern or half Asian. What if the person my mother "mixed" with was an abomination to her culture and then I find her and turn up on her doorstep, causing her unimaginable shame?'

Zack's face hardened. He looked away from me but held onto my hand so tightly he hurt me. 'I couldn't bear the rejection,' he said.

'Yet you reject God,' Pastor Michael said.

'I don't know him,' Zack replied. 'I can't see him.'

'Depends on how you look at things,' said Janice, softly, looking straight into Zack's eyes. 'Maybe he's always been there. The night your mother left you outside the orphanage, could he have led the woman that found you? Was there a plan for you being in the orphanage? Was it God who gave you your inner strength, so you would be strong for other people? Did he give you the ability to thrive and succeed in life against all odds? And the scholarship? And the ability to study law at university? Was it God who made a way for you to succeed in your career and other areas of your life? Zack, he's always been there.'

Zack's eyes filled with tears and he squeezed my hand again. 'He didn't stop *her* from killing my child.'

'He's given you another child to cherish and to love.'

Zack wept and I wept with him.

Saturday December 8

Listen to me, you who pursue righteousness and who seek the LORD: *Look to the rock from which you were cut (Isaiah 51:1).*

Today was Vanessa's wedding day and I was the seven months pregnant maid of honour. Think lump of lard and lilac and diaphanous gown and you'll have it.

The day went well. I finally came to face-to-face with the Sanctifieds and everyone else I'd tried so hard to avoid in the last few months. I thought they would whisper and nudge on seeing my bump and Zack by my side but they didn't. It was even good to see them. I thought that maybe, after all, it would be okay to start going back to church.

Watching Vanessa, all pink and white and beautiful, getting out of the shiny big car and taking her Dad's arm, I felt sort of sad. I was really, really wishing I'd waited like her. She was embarking on an adventure: marriage, sex, new job – in short, a whole new life. How I longed to be in her white satin shoes. She had chosen a better way. Instead of a new life, I'm trying to patch up an old one that keeps splitting open at the seams.

Following Vanessa down the aisle and watching her promises

with Mark, I reviewed all the bad decisions I'd made and now bitterly regretted. But, if I'd learned anything in all the counselling sessions, it was that God is a God of new beginnings. He only waits to forgive and accept us, to love us and bless us.

Along with all the other stuff crowding into my mind, I decided then and there that I was going to love this baby because it was a part of Zack and me. Just deciding to go through with giving birth wasn't enough. I would love and nurture our baby because it had a purpose here on earth just like we did. I determined to cherish this child because it's God's and because, through it and through God's grace, God is bringing Zack and me home to himself.

Monday February 4

But you brought my life up from the pit, O LORD my God (Jonah 2:6).

Zack and I had a beautiful baby boy this morning. It only took extreme loss of human dignity and 25 hours of excruciating labour but, hey, who's counting? His name is Yanis. It's a Hebrew name. It means God's gift. Zack chose it. His Nigerian name is Woboluwamitito. We're having the Nigerian naming ceremony in just over a week. My father is a modern man but there are some things he insists on. We've decided to call our son Yanis T for short. Mum says she will only call him by his full Nigerian name. After all, things must be done properly.

Within minutes of naming him, Zack was worrying about Yanis T.

'What about his race? What will he tick on questionnaires and forms that ask him his race? I don't want him to go through the same anxiety that I do.'

'He will tick "other". He's a half-Nigerian hybrid of Yoruba stock. He's also a representative of the Jesus Rainbow Coalition, otherwise known as the world.'

Before I forget, the Star Babies single *did* make the charts and *did* make the Christmas number one. Even Classic FM play it – occasionally. Windy CEO is full steam ahead for the World Star Baby competition to take place in about a year.

'And it will take place in Leeds. Not London. Not New York. Not Paris. Leeds. You just finish your maternity leave and come back. We're waiting for you.'

Oh, and yes, Zack proposed to me last week. We'd just finished watching *EastEnders* when he suddenly turned to me and said, bump notwithstanding, that I was the most beautiful woman in the world and would I marry him?

Of course, I said yes.

LEARN HOW TO MEET GOD THROUGH PRAYER AND BIBLE READING....

Making and growing a relationship with God is life-transforming. At the heart of Scripture Union's ministry is a desire to help people meet God and get to know him, and we produce many publications to encourage and help in this.

CLOSER TO GOD FOR NEWCOMERS: MEET THE REAL JESUS includes 40 brief excerpts taken from Luke's Gospel and the Book of Acts, with helpful insights. It describes Jesus' life and the effect he had on the people he met. It's straightforward, jargon-free and you don't need to know anything about Christianity to read it.

DAILY BREAD FOR NEW CHRISTIANS is an undated selection of readings and notes for anyone wanting to discover who Jesus is and what it means to follow him, how to make sense of the Bible, and how to understand the basics of the Christian faith.

Also recommended are:

AIRLOCK: an issues-based Bible reading series for young people.

CLOSER TO GOD: experiential, relational, radical and dynamic, this quarterly publication takes a creative and reflective approach to Bible reading.

DAILY BREAD: also quarterly, aiming to help you enjoy, explore and apply the Bible. Practical comments relate the Bible to everyday life.

For more information and advice:
• visit your local Christian bookshop
• phone SU's mail order line: 0845 0706006
• email info@scriptureunion.org.uk
• fax 01908 856020
• log on to www.scriptureunion.org.uk
• write to SU Mail Order, PO Box 5148, Milton Keynes MLO, MK2 2YX

STARTING POINTS –
USEFUL UK-BASED SOURCES OF HELP AND ADVICE

Acorn Pregnancy Counselling Centre
The Acorn Centre, Riverside, 1 Bond Street, Nuneaton, Coventry, CV11 5DA
Tel: 024 7638 1878
Fax: 024 7670 7401
Email: info@cswp.org.uk

Alternatives Pregnancy Counselling Centre
21–23 Clarendon Villas, Hove, East Sussex BN3 3RE
Tel: 01273 747687
www.cck.org.uk/Alternatives.asp

Choices Pregnancy Support
18 Cross Street, London N1 2BG
Tel: 0207 226 8590

Falkirk Pregnancy Crisis Centre
2 Glasgow Road, Camelon, Falkirk, FK1 4HJ
Tel: 0800 028 2228
Fax: 01324 628 583
Email: help@careconfidential.com

Christian Medical Fellowship
(For sound advice on medical issues and ethics)
CMF, Partnership House, 157 Waterloo Road, London SE1 8XN
Tel: 0207 928 4694
Fax: 0207 620 2453
Email: admin@cmf.org.uk
www.cmf.org.uk

Also:
www.careconfidential.com (will connect people to centres closest to them)
www.care-for-the-family.org.uk (will give advice on parenting/ being a single parent)
www.pregnancy.org.uk

MORE FICTION FROM SCRIPTURE UNION

Dear Bob by Annie Porthouse

Dear Bob,

Thought would write you, my future husband, diary re uni life. V much looking forward to meeting you. Prob you are super – Cn (Cliff Richard?) and hot bloke (maybe not...) and like Pringles, tiramisu, marriage...

Jude Singleton is about to face the biggest challenge of her life – she is looking for a man! On the way to finding 'Bob' she has to deal with those annoying distractions of university life: broken toes, waterproof curtains and driving instructors with dubious breath. Oh, and she's not sure whether there is a God, after all...

Love Jude by Annie Porthouse

Having survived her first year of uni, Jude Singleton has resolved some of her earlier spiritual difficulties. But will she be able to keep it all together when she finds a boyfriend?

The sequel continues Annie Porthouse's realistic look at student life and culture. Hilarious!

Letters to Kate by Claire Bankole

Looking at life with a God-perspective has its challenges. There's all the stuff around career and money. Confusing messages about sex and relationships. And, if you're trying to follow God, there's the added pressure of checking out if what you want to do is what he wants you to do!

Kate struggles, finding her way through the stressful and sometimes lonely transition from school to college, battling with burnout over exams, and coping with the huge demands of a year working overseas. It's great that she's not on her own. Claire's just a bit further on the journey. In sharing her own experiences, she gently guides Kate via letters, postcards and emails.

To order Scripture Union books:

- contact your local Christian bookshop
- phone SU's mail order line: 0845 0706006
- email info@scriptureunion.org.uk
- fax 01908 856020
- log on to www.scriptureunion.org.uk
- write to SU Mail Order, PO Box 5148, Milton Keynes MLO, MK2 2YX